Christmas for Lucy

A Child's Quest for Love

WELL OF LIFE
PUBLISHING

Christmas for Lucy

Christmas Hotel Series Book Two

by

Saundra Staats McLemore

Christmas for Lucy

A Child's Quest for Love

Christmas Hotel Series Book Two

By Saundra Staats McLemore

Paperback ISBN: 978-0-9826750-6-9
Also available as an eBook
eBook ISBN: 978-0-9826750-5-2
First published by
Desert Breeze Publishing 2013
© Saundra Staats McLemore 2013
This new and revised edition
© Saundra Staats McLemore 2019
Content Editor: Chris Wright
Cover Artist: J.L. Fuller
Photography Credit: Taria Reed Studios

Scripture Quotations are taken from the King James
Version of the Holy Bible

Published by
Well of Life Publishing
Ohio
United States of America

http://www.saundrastaatsmclemore.com

Other Books by Saundra Staats McLemore

The Staats Family Chronicles Series

Abraham and Anna – Book One of Staats Family Chronicles Series – Available now

Joy Out of Ashes

Book Two of Staats Family Chronicles Series

Available now

Christmas Hotel Series

Christmas Hotel (New edition)
Available November 22, 2018

Christmas for Lucy (New edition)
Available December 06, 2018

Christmas Redemption (New edition)
Available December 20, 2018

Christmas Pact (New edition)
Available October, 2019

Christmas Love and Mercy (New edition)
Available November, 2019

Christmas Hotel Reunion (New edition)
Available November, 2019

Dedication

Christmas for Lucy is dedicated to my son Gerald Anthony Staats. When he was born, he brought back the spirit of Christmas in my heart.

Acknowledgements

I would like to thank Joseph Palmer and Tony Staats for reading *Christmas for Lucy* and helping to find all those typos!

I thank Franklin, Kentucky historian, Gayla McClary Coates, for the needed information regarding Franklin, Kentucky in 1954 for *Christmas for Lucy*. She graciously answered my questions, and much of the information I was able to use for the accuracy of pertinent information in *Christmas for Lucy*.

I would like to offer a special thank you to Sid and Jill Broderson for granting me permission to have my characters Christopher and Jerilyn Wright and their children, reside in their historical home at 210 South College Street in Franklin, Kentucky. This beautiful home is known in Franklin as the *Montague House* or the *Malone House*. The Italianate structure was built around 1860 by William Clement Montague.

A special thank you to Barbara Beasley Smith and Martha James Thurmond for allowing me to have their fathers Dr. L. F. Beasley and Judge John James, Jr. "visit" the story.

As always, I thank my husband Robert E. McLemore for his complete support, as I enjoy the passion I have for writing.

I would like to thank our Lord and Savior, Jesus Christ for the inspiration He provides for every story I write.

But Jesus said, Suffer little children, and forbid them not, to come unto me: for of such is the kingdom of heaven.
Matthew 19:14

Chapters

Chapter One: Bullet 1

Chapter Two: The Old Man 7

Chapter Three: Mr. Gabe 11

Chapter Four: Christmas Hotel 22

Chapter Five: The First Night 29

Chapter Six: Shopping With Lucy 39

Chapter Seven: Forgiven Sins 44

Chapter Eight: Transitions 52

Chapter Nine: Uncle Otto and Aunt Eula Mae 57

Chapter Ten: Mr. Gabe's Cabin 66

Chapter Eleven: The Visitors 70

Chapter Twelve: The Sheriff 79

Chapter Thirteen: Homecoming for Lily 85

Chapter Fourteen: Family Time 90

Chapter Fifteen: The Sermon 104

Chapter Sixteen: The Long Drive 115

Chapter Seventeen: Compromise 121

Chapter Eighteen: Judge John James, Jr. 143

Chapter Nineteen: The Long Night 155

Chapter Twenty: The Letters 163

Chapter Twenty-One: Missing! 178

Chapter Twenty-Two: Christmas Hotel Chapel 194

Chapter Twenty-Three: Revelations 203

Chapter Twenty-Four: Family Love 213

Chapter Twenty-Five: The Long Awaited Children 224

Chapter Twenty-Six: Forgiveness 235

Chapter Twenty-Seven: Protector and Shield 242

Chapter Twenty-Eight: The Gift 248

Epilogue 257

About Saundra Staats McLemore 259

Author's Notes 261

Sneak Peek of *Christmas Redemption*

Book Three Christmas Hotel Series

Available December 20, 2018 264

Chapter One

Bullet

*"He shall cover thee with his feathers, and under
his wings shalt thou trust: his truth shall be thy
shield and buckler."*
Psalm 91:4

Bowling Green, Kentucky
9 pm Wednesday, December 1, 1954
Lucy lay curled in a ball near the fountain in
Fountain Square Park. The tears that had flowed so
freely earlier that day were now just dirty streaks
on her thin face. She gingerly tugged on the
threadbare coat to try to gain some warmth.
Although a hand-me-down from Hazel her older
cousin, for once Lucy was happy that the coat was
too big for her. She could wrap it around her body
like a blanket. However, the dress she wore was too
small, and the hem was well above her knees. She
wore Hazel's discarded boots, but no socks. Lucy
fled the apartment in such a hurry she forgot her
hat, scarf, and gloves.

Before she entered Fountain Square Park, she
stopped by the Methodist Church on State Street.
There was a Nativity scene out front, lit with

1

floodlights. She knelt by the manger that held the Baby Jesus. On occasion her mama attended this church along with Lucy, and even more often since August. Lucy knew about the Baby Jesus. Her Sunday school teacher Mrs. Scott taught her class about this precious baby. Mrs. Scott explained that He could save her from her sins and would protect her. Lucy did not understand sin, but she did understand the need for protection.

Lucy stared into the manger and studied the rubber doll representing the Baby Jesus and the statues of Mary and Joseph. Wrapped in a blanket, a sweet smile on the doll's face, and the statues of Mary and Joseph gazing on with love; the scene depicted what Lucy had been told about Jesus. Baby Jesus was loved. Lucy wanted to be loved.

She bowed her head and prayed aloud softly. "Dear Baby Jesus, I'm scared. Do You know my mama died this morning? Do You know today is my eighth birthday? Do You know that nobody cares about me? Do You know I'm all alone in the world? Do You know that I have no home? Will You help me, Baby Jesus? Will You protect me? Is there somebody out there who will love me? I'm so cold." As she prayed, the tears streamed down her face. No one came by. Lucy was indeed all alone.

The short, but poignant plea was prayed a couple of hours ago, and now Lucy lay shivering near the old fountain. Burying her head in her coat to seek as much warmth as possible, she resembled a scared turtle returning to the protection of its shell. She snuggled close to one of the shrubs around the fountain. The shrub provided some shelter, so at least she had a bit of protection from the cold damp air as she peered out from her coat and gazed up at the heavens. It was a clear evening, and she could see the stars. Her mama would tell her to count sheep in her head to go to sleep. Tonight she counted stars. With the leaves long gone from the park's trees, her eyes feasted on the clear view. By the time she counted approximately fifty stars, she was asleep.

In the middle of the night Lucy woke up shivering. In the shadows, a dog slowly walked toward her. Her heart beat faster in panic. Too frightened to run, she pulled her coat back over her head. If she couldn't see the dog, maybe he couldn't see her either. Feeling movement at her back, she tentatively peeped out from her coat. The dog, now lying down beside her, rested his head on her body. Cautiously, she reached out to pet him. He licked her hand and laid his huge head back down on her. Feeling safe with the dog, within fifteen minutes Lucy had stopped shivering and was asleep.

In those minutes just before the sun peaked over the horizon, she awakened. The dog still lay by her side, protecting her and warming her body. Sporting a rough, shaggy coat he was a good-sized dog and stretched out longer than Lucy. Her mama used to take her to Lerman's Department Store on the square where they sold the new televisions. Immediately after school, Lucy stopped on the way home, and also on Saturday morning when the store turned its television channel to The Roy Rogers Show. Every child in town, who didn't have a television, had his or her face pressed up against the store-front window. Bullet, Mr. Rogers's German Shepherd dog, and prominent in every episode, looked just like her new friend and protector. Lucy always wanted a dog, but her mama said they couldn't afford one, and had no space to keep one within their small apartment above *Tandy's Billiards.* Since this dog looked just like Bullet, she decided she'd call him Bullet. Remembering her prayer last night to the Baby Jesus, she said aloud, *"Thank You, Baby Jesus, for sending me Bullet."*

A light snow continued to fall. Thirsty, she stuck out her tongue to catch the snowflakes. Her mama told her she shouldn't drink the water in the fountain, because it was tainted. Bullet lifted his head and licked her cheek. She laughed and hugged him. Raising herself to a sitting position, she saw a man walking toward her in the dim morning light.

The man weaved along the walkway, stumbling every now and then. Holding a paper bag in one hand, he stopped long enough to bring the bag up to his mouth. When he was within ten feet of her, she could smell him. He smelled just like Uncle Otto and Aunt Eula Mae when they came home late at night. It was a sickening smell and Lucy didn't like her aunt and uncle when they had that smell. Sometimes they yelled at her or hit her. She stayed with them when her mama worked at night at the theater. They lived across the hall in an apartment over the billiard parlor, too.

The man stopped when he saw her, but did not come closer. A deep guttural growl in Bullet's throat grew louder and more menacing. The man stumbled away as quickly as possible, nearly tripping over his own feet. Lucy hugged Bullet to her. "Thank you, Bullet." She planted a big kiss on his massive head.

Lucy's stomach growled. She was hungry. She had not eaten since the previous morning, and even that was nothing substantial: just a piece of toast and some milk. She stood and Bullet stood beside her, tail wagging. He watched in anticipation of her next move. She looked to the east and had her first glimpse of the sun, just barely tipping above the horizon. Lucy stretched her arms, pulled her coat tighter, and looked around the park and the businesses on the square, but she saw no activity. She needed to relieve herself. There was a privy behind the billiard parlor and Lucy began to walk in that direction. Bullet followed.

When she returned to the park, she sat on the bench to view the fountain and wait; however, she really had no idea why she was waiting. As she stroked Bullet's head, she spoke aloud. "Mama, why did you have to die?"

She looked up to the heavens and the tears began again.

Chapter Two

The Old Man

"For I the LORD thy God will hold thy right hand,
saying unto thee, Fear not; I will help thee."
Isaiah 41:13

Thursday morning
December 2, 1954
Lucy wiped her tears on the sleeve of her coat.
Hearing the clip-clop sound of a horse's hooves on
the pavement, she turned her head to see an old
man driving an even older farm wagon pulled by
one horse. Cautiously rising from the bench, she
stared at the sight. Nowadays, people rode in their
truck or automobile to town, unless of course they
were within walking distance. She had never seen a
horse-drawn farm wagon in town. As far as she
knew, no farmers still used them.

The old man waved at her, and she warily
returned his wave; unsure about approaching the
man, but not wanting to be rude either. She looked
down at the dog. "What do you think, Bullet?"

The old man was now about fifty feet from
where she stood in the park. "Whoa, ol' Bob," he
said, tugging on the reins. Lucy stood transfixed as

he pulled up on the parking brake, then stepped down from the wagon and walked toward her. This time Bullet did not growl. Bullet ran and greeted the stranger affectionately, jumping up and placing his front paws on the old man's shoulders, licking him square in the face. When standing on his hind legs, the dog stood as tall as the man.

The man roughed the fur on Bullet's neck and scratched him behind the ears. He walked to Lucy with Bullet hopping at his heels. Lucy scrutinized the old man. He had a long gray beard, was mostly bald on his head, wearing overalls with a red and black plaid flannel shirt. His overcoat was unbuttoned, and it appeared to be made from deer hide. He wore heavy boots.

"Hello, young lady, what brings you out so early in the morning?"

Lucy followed his eyes as he looked down at her legs. The shrubs must have scratched them last night. She had not even noticed the small amount of blood that seeped from the scratches.

"Is your mama nearby to put some antiseptic on those scratches?"

Lucy looked down at the ground and nervously shifted from one foot to the other. She didn't know what to say to the man, but she knew she didn't want to cry. There was no one else around. Her aunt and uncle didn't want her. Her cousins just made fun of her. Looking back up at the man, she saw a kind face, and she took her cue from Bullet. She decided to trust him.

When she finally spoke, her voice was barely audible. "My mama's dead."

He knelt in front of her, placing one hand on her shoulder. "I'm sorry, child. What about your father?"

"I never met my father. Mama said he died before I was born."

"Any other kinfolk?"

Raising her chin, she blinked back any tears that threatened to spill over. With a quiver in her chin she replied, "No one that wants me."

Lucy looked into his faded blue eyes and saw compassion.

"What's your name, child?"

"Lucy Clark."

The old man petted Bullet. "What's your friend's name?"

"I call him Bullet ... sir," she added after a short pause. Lucy knew she had been forgetting her manners.

"Are you hungry?"

"Yes, sir."

"It just so happens that I am, too. I live in a small cabin down the road a ways. I'm sure I can scrounge us up something to eat. Would you and

Bullet like to have breakfast with me?"

Lucy thought for a moment. Her mama had always told her to never go anywhere with strangers. She thought about Bullet's earlier response to the man who had smelled of alcohol. She knew Bullet did not like him, and he made sure the man did not come near her. However, his reaction to this man was different. She decided to trust Bullet's instincts. She liked the man, too. "Yes, sir, we would like to have breakfast with you."

"Well, let's get going, Lucy. You can sit up on the bench seat with me, and Bullet can jump in the back."

He wrapped a patchwork quilt around Lucy, and as they pulled away from the square, Lucy looked up at the apartments above *Tandy's Billiards*. The faded curtain at her aunt's apartment was pulled back, and she saw the shadow of a face at the window. The face quickly vanished and the curtain closed. She turned herself to the road ahead and squared her thin little shoulders. There was no one up in that apartment that cared about her.

Chapter Three

Mr. Gabe

*"In the fear of the LORD is strong confidence: and
his children shall have a place of refuge."*
Proverbs 14:26

December 2 and 3, 1954
On a rare occasion, her mama drove her along this
road into Franklin, Kentucky, and she liked looking
at all the different farm houses and the farm
animals. If her mama had some extra money, they
would have the noon meal at Christmas Hotel. To
Lucy, Christmas Hotel was the grandest place in the
whole world. She wondered if they would later go to
Franklin. She hoped so.

After driving a few miles, the man pulled his
wagon onto an old gravel road leading back to a
small cabin. The outside of the cabin was rustic, but
well-tended with closed shutters on each window.
Lucy saw neatly arranged flower beds that due to
winter only held shrubs. Cattle grazed on the winter
grass in the field behind the barn. The man reined
in the horse and set the parking brake. Bullet leapt
over the sidewall of the wagon and headed into the
woods.

The old man chuckled. "I imagine he caught scent of a rabbit. Don't worry; he'll be back as soon as he's eaten his breakfast."

Relieved at his comment, she let out the breath she'd been holding.

The man climbed down from the wagon, lifted Lucy to the ground and unharnessed the horse. He walked the horse to a fenced-in area near the cabin and closed the gate. Lucy watched as the horse began to graze on the winter grass. The old man headed to the front door with Lucy close on his heels. He opened the door, and they both stepped inside.

High ceilings and floor to ceiling windows accented the architecture of the homey interior of the cabin's living room. There wasn't a lot of furniture – just two rocking chairs in front of the fireplace, a sofa along one wall, an antique oak table between the rocking chairs, and a coffee table in front of the sofa. A large braided rug nearly covered the highly polished hard wood floors. Two newspapers lay on the coffee table: one from Bowling Green and one from Franklin, both dated from the previous week.

A portrait of a lovely woman hung over the fireplace and landscape pictures adorned the walls in the front room. Pre-cut firewood, brush and twigs had been neatly stacked beside the fireplace.

The man looked up the chimney to make certain the flue was open and lay a pile of twigs and brush in the fireplace. He pulled a Diamond matchbox from his pocket, struck a match, and cupped the flame with his other hand. He lit the small pile of brush and began to lightly blow on it. Soon the twigs ignited and he added a small dry log. They now had a nice roaring fire. They both stood in front of the fire a few minutes to warm their bodies.

In the rear of the cabin, a large oak table that would easily seat six took up most of the open space in the middle of the kitchen. An ice box, oak pie safe, a huge oak cupboard with sparkling glasses and pretty and decorative dishes, and an iron wood stove lined three walls, along with pictures of Bowling Green businesses, landscapes, and a painting of Christmas Hotel.

Opening a door in the cupboard, he removed antiseptic and cotton. He asked Lucy to sit at the kitchen table while he cleaned the scratches on her legs. "There you go, Lucy. That should keep any infection away."

He opened the three-door ice box. The iceman must have been there earlier, because there was a large block in the top compartment. The man grabbed a glass from the cupboard, opened the spigot on the icebox, and drew a glass of water. He offered it to Lucy who immediately accepted it.

"Thank you, sir," Lucy said, and drank thirstily.

"Slow down, Lucy! Not so fast."

He asked Lucy to remain seated at the table. Beside the iron wood stove, more cut firewood was neatly stacked. He loaded twigs, a couple of pre-cut logs, and some of the newspaper in the front room into the stove, lit it, and closed the door. The iron on the stove was black and shiny as though it had recently been rubbed with lard. Within minutes, the kitchen was also warm. Using lye soap and water from the pump by the sink, he scrubbed the top of the old oak table. Opening another door in the cupboard, he removed flour, baking powder, baking soda, salt, and a measuring cup. Mixing the proper amounts together, he rubbed in some butter and shortening. He whistled Christmas songs while he worked, and Lucy sang along to "Rudolph the Red-Nosed Reindeer."

Lucy watched spellbound as the man worked. She'd never seen someone work so hard in the kitchen, and all for her. In her experience, women did the cooking, not men. "Lucy, please bring me a bottle of buttermilk from the icebox." She dutifully did as he asked. Pouring in some buttermilk, he stirred until the dough came together and was sticky.

He lightly floured the oak table, rolled the dough onto it, dusted the top with flour, and using a rolling pin, rolled the dough over and over several times. He then pressed out the dough until it was about an inch thick, selected a glass from the cupboard, and cut out the dough to the appropriate size. He placed the round dough pieces on a baking sheet he had greased with lard, and pushed the sheet into the oven of the woodstove. He again scrubbed the table.

Setting an iron skillet on the burner, he added bacon that had been stored in the icebox. When the bacon was finished frying, he wrapped it in a clean towel and set the bacon beside the stove, allowing the grease to absorb in the towel. Pulling out another iron skillet, he added some of the bacon grease to it, a couple of tablespoons of the flour, along with some salt and pepper, and stirred it all together.

"Lucy, would you bring me the bottle of sweet milk from the icebox, please?"

She did as instructed and watched as the old man stirred it into the iron skillet. As the gravy thickened, he asked Lucy to bring him four eggs from the icebox. By now Lucy's mouth had begun to water, and her stomach growled again. He cracked the eggs on the side of the first skillet, and dropped them in. Lucy listened as the eggs crackled and popped, and the man returned to the other skillet and stirred the gravy.

"Lucy, if you'll set the table with dinnerware, napkins, plates, and a glass of milk for each of us, I'll serve up the food. Oh, and please grab a jar of strawberry preserves from the pantry in that room." He pointed to a closed door in the corner.

Lucy did as instructed, and now her stomach was really growling. After she set the table, she watched as he served the biscuits, gravy, bacon, and eggs. She could not remember when she had had such a splendid meal.

They both sat down at the table. She wanted to dive right in, but the man gently touched her arm and stopped her. "We must thank our Lord for the food."

Lucy bowed her head.

"Dear Heavenly Father, we thank Thee for the food that Thou hast provided. We thank Thee for Thy Son Jesus for salvation. We thank Thee for protecting our little Lucy. Let her know that Thou art in control and that Thou wilt provide for her future. In the name of Jesus we pray, amen."

Lucy politely waited for the man to pick up his fork and then she followed. She gulped the food because she was so hungry. "Slow down, Lucy. You'll make yourself sick, or choke. There's plenty of food." He smiled as he spoke, so she knew he wasn't upset with her.

She finally had her fill and thanked the man for

the meal. She had been wondering how to ask him his name, and finally got up the nerve to say, "You know my name, but I don't know yours."

He leaned back in his chair, thoughtfully stroking his long gray beard. "My name is Gabriel, but you may call me Gabe."

Lucy smiled. "I would not be allowed ... I mean, that is, if my mama was still alive ... to call you Gabe, but I can call you Mr. Gabe ... if that's all right with you."

He chuckled, "Mr. Gabe is fine with me."

They both turned when they heard a scratching at the back door. Mr. Gabe rose and opened the door. Bullet entered, and they laughed when they saw the rabbit fur around his muzzle.

"Well, I guess Bullet got his breakfast, too!" Mr. Gabe said, still laughing.

Bullet hurried to Lucy and she hugged him. "I love you, Bullet. Thank you for coming back to me," she said, wrapping her scrawny little arms around him and burying her face in the fur around his neck.

As soon as breakfast was finished, Lucy helped Mr. Gabe with the chores. He had cows to milk, and under his supervision she also mucked out the stalls and added the fresh straw. When that was done, they put fresh water and feed in the troughs. Later that day, Lucy rode one of Mr. Gabe's ponies, a cream colored Shetland. "It's just the perfect size for me!" She laughed as Mr. Gabe led the pony around the paddock.

"She has no name, so would you like to choose a name for her, Lucy?"

Lucy thought long and hard. Finally her face brightened. "Millie! I want to call her Millie, the same as the comic book I like to read."

Mr. Gabe laughed. "Okay, Millie will be her name. A pretty name for a pretty pony."

After supper, Mr. Gabe read aloud from the Bible, while Bullet lay at Lucy's feet. He also read her the newly published children's book, *The Happy Lion*. There were no books in Lucy's home. Occasionally, her mama took her to the library. Her mama had to work ... a lot. Lucy spent the majority of her evenings with her aunt, uncle, and four cousins. They mostly ignored her, and Lucy did her best to steer clear of them.

Lucy and Bullet spent the night in Mr. Gabe's spare bedroom. When Lucy lived with her mama, they only had three rooms: one for their living room, one for their kitchen, and one for their shared bedroom, along with a tiny bathroom. There was not much money, so pretty pillows and rugs in the rooms and nice furniture did not exist, but this was a beautifully decorated little room with frilly curtains at the windows and a patchwork quilt on the white iron bed, loaded with colorful pillows. A rocking chair with bright blue and pink printed cushions sat in the corner and a fluffy pink rug covered the rustic southern pine floor. It was a little girl's dream room.

Lucy and Mr. Gabe knelt beside the bed. Mr. Gabe said a prayer for Lucy and then Lucy said her prayer aloud. "Dear God, thank You for Bullet. He kept me warm. He kept me from being so lonely. He watched over me. Thank You for my new friend Mr. Gabe. He's a nice man. God bless Bullet and Mr. Gabe... amen." Lucy climbed into bed, and Mr. Gabe tucked her in.

"Good night, little one. I wish you nothing but sweet dreams beginning tonight." He petted Bullet on the head, and the dog lay on the floor by Lucy's bed. Within minutes Lucy was sound asleep.

The next morning, Lucy heard Mr. Gabe in the kitchen cooking breakfast, and she joined him after letting Bullet outside. Mr. Gabe set oatmeal, honey, milk, orange slices, toast, butter, and jam on the table. He sat beside Lucy, and they held hands as he asked the blessing.

They were quiet for a few minutes and then Mr. Gabe spoke. "You need someone to take care of you, Lucy. I know of a family in Franklin that can help. I think they are the ones to decide your future."

She looked at him wide-eyed with

apprehension.

"Don't worry, Lucy. I have not met them personally, but I have been told they are very nice people. How old are you, child?"

"I turned eight two days ago. That was also the day my mama died," she said, as she bowed her head. Her lip began to tremble and there was a catch in her voice.

"Oh, child, don't cry. Try to be brave. This couple has three children: a girl of eighteen, and a twin boy and girl age twelve. I will drive you there after breakfast. They're the owners of a place called Christmas Hotel. It's a place where the birth of Jesus Christ is celebrated every day."

Lucy looked up at him with a big smile. "I've been there with my mama! When she had extra money, we would go there for our noon meal. I love Christmas Hotel!" Bullet scratched at the kitchen door wanting in. "What about Bullet? Can he come, too?" she asked in a concerned voice.

Mr. Gabe rose and let Bullet in. The dog ran straight to Lucy. She put her arms around him and hugged him close.

"I don't see why we can't take him. Let's not fret. Things have a way of working out."

Lucy helped Mr. Gabe clean up the kitchen. He put out the fires in the kitchen stove and the fireplace, and closed the front door. After hitching

Ol' Bob to the farm wagon, Mr. Gabe helped Lucy up on the front seat. He climbed up on the other side, while Bullet jumped into the rear. He released the brake and they headed down the road to Franklin.

Chapter Four

Christmas Hotel

*"Be not forgetful to entertain strangers: for
thereby some have entertained angels unawares."*
Hebrews 13:2

Friday, December 3, 1954
Late morning Franklin, KY
Lucy had not been to Franklin when it was
decorated for Christmas, so the town was more
beautiful than she remembered. Bulbs and
twinkling lights adorned the trees in the square. All
the light posts had been wrapped with garland with
a red bow attached at the top, and the doors of the
businesses around the square were decorated with
wreaths.

Mr. Gabe parked the horse and wagon along
East Cedar Street beside Christmas Hotel, and
helped Lucy down. Bullet followed, shadowing
them as Mr. Gabe held Lucy's hand and led her to
the park bench across North Main Street that faced
the front door of Christmas Hotel. Bullet relieved
himself, and then sprawled on the ground when
Mr. Gabe and Lucy seated themselves on the bench.

They both looked across North Main Street at the hotel.

Christmas Hotel was an amazing structure: five stories tall and built in the Italianate style architecture. CHRISTMAS HOTEL was carved into a massive stone block near the top of the fifth story, and just below this, Lucy could see another carving, also in stone: WHERE JESUS' BIRTH IS A DAILY CELEBRATION. The massive double glass doors, two stories high, were recessed about twenty inches into the building. Gas coach lights shone warmly from above the stone angels carved into the facade on each side of the double doors.

"Lucy, I'd like for you to wait here with Bullet while I go inside and explain your situation. I'll be right back, so don't worry. Will you promise to wait here with Bullet for me to return?"

"Yes, Mr. Gabe, I promise."

He patted Lucy's arm and rose from the bench. Lucy watched him cross the street and enter Christmas Hotel.

He was only gone about ten minutes when he reappeared at the door. Mr. Gabe waited for a car to pass, and then motioned for her and Bullet to come. Lucy and Bullet entered through one of the massive double brass trimmed glass doors. The first thing Lucy saw was the immense Christmas tree in the center of the lobby, and the life-size Nativity set nestled in the horseshoe shaped grand staircase. A man and woman sat side-by-side on a sofa near the tree. They stood as Lucy entered the room with Mr. Gabe. Mr. Gabe held her hand to escort her over to the couple, with Bullet walking close at Lucy's heels.

Mr. Gabe made the introductions. "Miss Lucy, I would like for you to meet Mr. and Mrs. Wright."

Lucy politely curtsied. "I'm pleased to meet you both."

They each extended a hand to shake Lucy's hand. Mr. Wright responded for them both. "We're very pleased to meet you, too, Lucy. Please sit with us so we can talk."

Mr. Gabe and Lucy sat on the sofa across from the Wrights, and Bullet sat on the floor beside Lucy.

Mr. Wright spoke first. "Mr. Gabe told us a little about your situation, Lucy. We understand your mama died two days ago, and you have no kinfolk to take care of you." He paused for Lucy to respond.

"Yes, sir."

"We are very sorry. You have our condolences."

"Thank you, sir," she answered demurely.

"Are you in school?" asked Mrs. Wright.

"I was until last week. Mama made sure I went to school every day. I'm in the third grade."

"Where did you live with your mama?" continued Mrs. Wright.

Mrs. Wright closely watched Lucy's face, as she answered the questions. "We lived in Bowling Green in an apartment above *Tandy's Billiards*. It's across from Fountain Square Park." Nervously picking at the threads on her coat, Lucy kicked her legs, dangling off the sofa; anxiously awaiting a decision, not only for her, but also for Bullet.

Mr. Wright turned to Lucy, and resumed the questions. "Lucy, you must still have clothes at the apartment and your mama's personal items. Have you been back to retrieve them?"

"No, sir. My aunt, uncle, and cousins live in the apartment across the hall. When Mama didn't wake up, I went to Aunt Eula Mae for help. As soon as Aunt Eula Mae saw Mama was dead, she told me to get out. She said she and Uncle Otto didn't want another mouth to feed."

A look of horror crossed Mrs. Wright's face, and Lucy overheard Mrs. Wright whisper to her husband that she couldn't imagine anyone being so cruel, let alone family. She appeared to be struggling to hold back the anger.

Mr. Wright took his wife's hand. "I'm sorry, Lucy," Mrs. Wright managed to say. "We want you to stay with us until we can decide what to do about your future. Will that be all right with you?"

"Yes, ma'am," Lucy answered. "What about Bullet?" she asked uneasily, looking down at Bullet and petting him.

Mr. Wright smiled and nodded. "Bullet can stay, too. He looks like he's quite attached to you, and he seems friendly."

"Oh, he is, Mr. Wright!" Then she remembered the man at the park who smelled of alcohol, and quickly added, "He did growl one time at a man who came near me at the park. I don't think Bullet liked him, but he didn't growl at Mr. Gabe. Bullet knew right away that Mr. Gabe was a nice man!"

Mr. Wright chuckled. "Well, it appears as though Bullet is quite discerning. I think we need a smart dog like Bullet around Christmas Hotel."

Lucy jumped up and hugged both the Wrights. "Oh, thank you, Mr. Wright and Mrs. Wright! We'll be so good. I promise, you won't even know we're here!"

Christopher smiled and shook his head. "You don't have to go that far, Lucy. It'll be nice having a younger child in the house again. Our three children are older."

Mr. Gabe rose. "Well, I suppose I have accomplished my mission, so I'll be going." He shook hands with the Wrights, and then hugged Lucy and petted Bullet.

He was out the door before Lucy remembered her manners. "I must go thank him!" she said, running to the door with Bullet close behind. Mr.

and Mrs. Wright followed. Lucy tugged on the heavy door in vain, and Mr. Wright reached around Lucy and pulled it open.

The Wrights followed Lucy and Bullet as they ran around the corner onto East Cedar Street. When they rounded the corner they found Lucy and Bullet just standing there. Lucy turned to them in dismay. "Mr. Gabe parked his wagon here. His horse Ol' Bob was hitched to the wagon. They're gone!"

"Lucy, are you sure this is where Mr. Gabe parked?" asked Mrs. Wright.

"I'm positive. They ... just disappeared! I didn't get to say goodbye. I didn't get to thank him." She felt a tear trickling down her cheek.

Mrs. Wright looked at Mr. Wright and then bent down to comfort Lucy, placing her arms around her.

"I don't understand," continued Lucy. "Where could he have gone so quickly?"

Mrs. Wright looked over Lucy's shoulder up at Mr. Wright. "I don't know, honey," and she held Lucy closer. "Let's all go back inside and get warm."

As they walked back inside, Lucy noticed Mrs. Wright shooting Mr. Wright a puzzled look. He returned the look and simply shrugged his shoulders, moved his head from side-to-side, as though acknowledging he was confused, too, and held his hands palms up. He mouthed the words, "I don't know," to Mrs. Wright, but loudly enough for Lucy to hear.

Opening the door to Christmas Hotel, they all stepped inside. The Wrights appeared to be deep in thought about what just happened, and Lucy wondered what the next step to help her would be – assuming they were going to help her.

Chapter Five

The First Night

"For God, who commanded the light to shine out of darkness, hath shined in our hearts, to give the light of the knowledge of the glory of God in the face of Jesus Christ."
2 Corinthians 4:6

Friday evening
December 3, 1954
Lucy and Bullet spent the latter part of the afternoon in room #7 at Christmas Hotel, with the twelve-year-old twins Kenneth Elliot and Carrie Emeline. After hearing Lucy's story, Jerilyn and Christopher proudly looked on as their children befriended Lucy. On school days, Ken and Carrie Emeline did their homework in room #7, and ate dinner with their parents in the hotel's dining room before the whole family went home for the evening. Today they invited Lucy to join them while they completed their homework.

Room #7 held a special significance for Jerilyn. Thirteen years ago, on December 7, 1941, her first husband died at Pearl Harbor. The distraught Jerilyn left her home in Dayton, Ohio with the

29

intentions of meeting her husband's family in Nashville and hopefully finding employment. Along the way, someone had stolen her purse, and she did not realize it until a train stop in Franklin, Kentucky. She was widowed, penniless, pregnant, and alone. She did not know how to pray, and thought God had left her because she had left Him.

Jerilyn remained in Franklin, Kentucky at Christmas Hotel in room #7. She found a diary from 1883 that had belonged to a twenty-year-old girl. The girl wrote about her fiancé Seth who took a position with the railroad, and was killed coupling railroad cars. The girl blamed God for Seth's death. Jerilyn had instantly felt a kinship with her, because she too blamed God for her husband's death. However, after a while, the girl's feelings changed and so did Jerilyn's. Eventually, the young girl, whose name was Carrie Emeline, asked the Lord to forgive her, and Jerilyn also asked for forgiveness. It was in room #7 that Jerilyn rededicated her life to the Lord. Jerilyn married Christopher, and gave birth to her first husband's twins four months later.

Jerilyn and Christopher concluded their work at the hotel for the day, and instead of dinner in the dining room they decided to head home with the four children. They could not allow Bullet in Christmas Hotel's dining room, and the dog did not want to leave Lucy. They could tell he was very protective of Lucy. Therefore, the family left Christmas Hotel and walked the short distance home.

As they ambled along, Lucy's eyes darted around the four blocks of the square, relishing in all the sights. The square reminded her of the one in Bowling Green with all the businesses surrounding it. There was no big fountain, but it was still just as beautiful. Darkness had now settled on the town. During past Christmases, Lucy did fun things with her mama. They would go shopping in all the pretty stores and decorate a tree in their tiny apartment. December was the only month they attended church each week. However, this Christmas would be very different. She had no mama, and her mama's family didn't want her.

The five of them turned from the sidewalk to the brick walkway leading up to the home at 210 South College Street. The family lived in a two-story pale yellow frame home with deep green shutters and a dark brown roof. Six steps led up to the entrance and by the front door, and an oak sign below one of the two lanterns read: The Wright Family. In the window to the left of the front door, a Christmas tree twinkled brightly.

Lucy stared in awe. She could not believe she was entering such a grand home. Mr. Wright unlocked the door and they all stepped inside. A dog slowly limped toward them in greeting. The dog was not frisky, so Lucy rightly assumed the animal was old. Bullet walked in beside Lucy and the two dogs greeted as dogs do.

Ken turned to Lucy. "This is our dog Daisy. She's almost fifteen, so she's not very active, but she'll still shake hands with you if you ask her." He turned to Daisy and commanded, "Sit, Daisy." The dog obediently sat in front of him. "Now you can say, 'Daisy shake,' and she'll shake your hand."

Lucy walked up to Daisy. "Daisy, shake." Daisy slowly raised her paw and Lucy shook it while laughing with excitement. "I think she likes me!" she giggled in delight.

Mrs. Wright smiled at Lucy. "Lucy, it makes my heart glad to hear you laughing. By the way, Lucy, since we're friends, I think you can call Mr. Wright and me Mr. Christopher and Mrs. Jerilyn. Okay?"

Lucy's smile widened. "Thank you, Mrs. Jerilyn! I'd like that."

Mrs. Jerilyn addressed Carrie Emeline. "Why don't you take Lucy upstairs to the guestroom? Look in the trunk and you'll find some clothes you've outgrown. Please take her to the bathroom to bathe and change clothes, while I cook dinner. Help her wash her hair while she's in the tub. In the meantime, I'm sure your dad and brother would delight in taking Bullet to the basement for a bath." Mrs. Jerilyn looked at Mr. Christopher with a smile and a wink.

One hour later the family reassembled in the dining room with both dogs lying on the rug in the living room in front of the fireplace. The family and Lucy held hands while Mr. Christopher asked the blessing. "Dear Heavenly Father, we thank Thee for this dinner Thou hast provided and we thank Thee for bringing Lucy to us." Lucy was seated beside him and he squeezed her hand. "She's a very special young lady and we ask for Thy divine assistance to help Lucy with her future. We ask this in the name of Thy Son Jesus ... amen."

The family added their amens.

As they passed around the meal of left-over fried chicken, green beans, biscuits, mashed potatoes, and gravy, Mr. Christopher began the conversation. "How was school today?"

Carrie Emeline responded first. "I received an A-plus on my history test! I was worried I wouldn't remember all the dates, but I did."

Ken answered next, "I got an A on my science test. I wasn't too worried about that, but I was nervous about the history. I got a C on the history."

"What did you get on your science test, Carrie Emeline?" asked Mr. Christopher.

She hung her head. "I didn't do as well on that. I

received a C-minus. I try, but science is so hard for me."

"As long as you did your best, that's all that matters. Maybe Ken can help you get the science grade up and you can work with him on history. Lily will be home for Christmas in a couple of weeks. I'm sure she'll assist both of you." Mr. Christopher turned to Lucy and explained, "Lily is our older daughter and she's away at college in Lexington at the University of Kentucky. She plans on teaching grade school when she's graduated."

Lucy watched as the family ate and conversed, politely and naturally. Yes, it would be wonderful to be part of a big, united family. She sat silently as at times they laughed and teased each other. Lucy had never known her father, and did not understand how a family interacted, but she felt the love and affection surrounding these people. She had loved her mama, but had only been shown loathing by the others in her family. Was this how most families lived ... and loved? She was deep in thought and did not hear her name at first.

"Lucy," said Mrs. Jerilyn, obviously a second time, but she spoke in a kind voice.

Lucy looked up at her. "I'm sorry, Mrs. Jerilyn. Did you ask me a question?"

"I just wanted to say that tomorrow is Saturday. Carrie Emeline and I go into town most Saturdays to buy groceries and check the sales at all the shops on the square. If Bullet will stay with Ken, maybe you would like to go with us. We can also go shopping for a dress and some shoes for you to wear to church on Sunday. When we're finished, we girls can have our noon meal at Christmas Hotel. Would you like that?"

Lucy's face brightened. Very softly she simply replied, "Yes, ma'am."

Later that evening, Lucy and Carrie Emeline sat in the guestroom where Lucy would sleep. The house had five bedrooms, and the other four were occupied by the family. Although Lily was away at school, Mrs. Jerilyn had explained that Lily's room was kept just for her when she was home. In Lucy's opinion, the guestroom was beautiful, with a huge cherry four-poster bed, an oak marble top dresser, a lovely vanity with a blue and white skirt fitted around it, and a Singer sewing machine with some material left in it. A small corner bookshelf held several books and magazines, and family photos adorned the walls and dresser. Carrie Emeline asked Lucy to choose a book while she went to fetch a nightgown for Lucy to wear.

Mrs. Jerilyn stood in the doorway, but Lucy was aware Mrs. Jerilyn was watching her look over the books. "Lucy," Mrs. Jerilyn said softly, "my heart goes out to you. There was a time when I knew what it was like to be frightened and alone. However, the Lord had a plan for my future. I know the Lord has a plan for you, too."

Lucy wiped a tear because of the kindness shown by a stranger, and not wanting Mrs. Jerilyn to see her face, she kept her head turned away while she scanned the bookshelf.

Soon Carrie Emeline returned with the nightgown, and she helped Lucy change for bed. Mrs. Jerilyn picked up a brush on the vanity table, and they all three climbed onto the bed. Mrs. Jerilyn brushed Lucy's long brown curls. Carrie Emeline began to read the book Lucy had chosen – a book that Lucy was told, Mrs. Jerilyn purchased earlier in the year, a new version of *The Little Engine That Could.*

When Carrie Emeline finished reading the short inspirational story, Jerilyn asked both girls what they learned from the book.

Carrie Emeline was the first to answer. After mulling over her answer, she closed her eyes and with her hands folded over the still open book, she said, "I can hear my favorite Bible verse every time the little engine struggles to pull the freight cars up the hill. The little engine keeps repeating, 'I think I can, I think I can, I think I can.' Later as he makes it to the top of the hill, he says, 'I thought I could, I thought I could, I thought I could.' The little engine realizes he can do it, and that's what I think of Philippians 4: 13: '*I can do all things through Christ which strengtheneth me.*'" She opened her eyes, looked at her mother, and smiled. "I think of the importance of knowing I can accomplish anything; principles that you and Daddy have taught Lily, Ken, and me." She shot Mrs. Jerilyn a wry smile. "I know I can, I know I can, I know I can get my science grade up to an A."

Mrs. Jerilyn laughed and hugged her daughter. Turning to Lucy she asked, "What did you learn from the story?"

Lucy stared down at her lap where she was wringing her hands together. She looked up at Mrs. Jerilyn, aware her voice sounded tiny as she said, "I learned that if I try really hard, I will not feel so sad, and that someday my family might want me."

Mrs. Jerilyn embraced Lucy. "I want that, honey ... I want that, too." Mrs. Jerilyn closed her eyes and whispered, "*Help her, Lord,*" Over Mrs. Jerilyn's shoulder, Lucy saw the tears running down Carrie Emeline's face.

Carrie Emeline quickly wiped the tears away, and Mrs. Jerilyn released Lucy. Carrie Emeline glanced around the guestroom. "Lucy, this room is lovely, but maybe you don't want to sleep alone. Would you like to sleep in my room tonight? I have twin beds. We can tell stories until we fall asleep, and then neither one of us will be lonely." Lucy looked at Carrie Emeline. "I'd like that. Can Bullet sleep on the floor?"

"I have no problem with Bullet sleeping on the floor, especially now that he's had a bath!"

With that statement, all three laughed, and the tension was dispelled.

Carrie Emeline grabbed Lucy's hand and they continued laughing as they ran down the hall to Carrie Emeline's bedroom. Before they left the room, Lucy overheard Mrs. Jerilyn praying quietly, "Dear Lord, I thank You for my compassionate daughter. She's just what Lucy needed tonight."

Chapter Six

Shopping With Lucy

"Ye are of God, little children, and have overcome them: because greater is he that is in you, than he that is in the world."
1 John 4:4

Saturday morning
December 4, 1954

The family was up early Saturday morning. From the trunk, Carrie Emeline chose an outgrown dress to fit Lucy, and some shoes, and the three of them were out the door at eight o'clock. They first drove to the *Piggly Wiggly* grocery store. When they finished their grocery shopping, and before returning home, Jerilyn drove back to the square, parked the car, and hurried into the *Blue Rose Bakery*, leaving the girls in the car.

Lucy did not have a birthday cake on her birthday, and although it was three days past her birthday, Jerilyn intended for her to have one tonight. She ordered a two-layer chocolate cake with white icing, and she requested HAPPY BIRTHDAY, LUCY to be written on top.

Dropping off their groceries at home, they then

headed out again on foot to *Gillespie Dry Goods.* Mr. Gillespie had plenty of yard goods along with some dresses already made. Jerilyn and Carrie Emeline picked out five dresses, a winter coat, a fur muff, shoes, boots, hat, scarf, mittens, socks, and underclothes for Lucy.

Lucy was so excited. "I've never been shopping for new clothes. Everything I ever owned was 'hand-me-down.' With each dress she tried on, Lucy whirled in front of the mirror and shrieked with laughter, while Jerilyn and Carrie Emeline told her how pretty she was. Lucy's bright blue eyes sparkled and her dimples danced when she laughed.

They delivered the packages home, before walking to the other side of the square to Christmas Hotel. When they arrived on the corner of East Cedar and North Main Street, Lucy turned her head to the right down South Main Street to the Roxy Theater. *White Christmas* was featured starring Bing Crosby and Rosemary Clooney.

"Lucy, have you been to many movies?" asked Carrie Emeline.

"When Mama had the time," answered Lucy. "She worked a lot. She sold the movie tickets at the State Theater on the square in Bowling Green. If she wasn't working on Saturday morning we would go see a movie. The manager gave us free tickets. I really like the Tweety Bird cartoons and the Disney movies. I cried when Bambi's mama died." Lucy looked down at the sidewalk and used the toe of her shoe to move an imaginary object. Jerilyn placed her arm around Lucy realizing she was probably remembering her own mama.

"Mom, maybe when Lily gets home we can all go see *White Christmas*," said Carrie Emeline.

"I think that's a wonderful idea. What do you think, Lucy?"

She looked up at them and merely said in a quiet voice, "I'd like that."

"Well, it's a date then. I'm sure the men would like to see it, too." Jerilyn took the hands of both girls and entered Christmas Hotel, and the weekend doorman opened and held the heavy door. The weekends were always the busiest, so many years ago they employed the doorman. The guests liked the added touch, too.

"Good afternoon, Mrs. Wright," he greeted her, and tipped his hat.

"Good afternoon, Charles. I'd like you to meet our new friend Lucy."

"Good afternoon, Miss Lucy."

"Good afternoon, Mr. Charles," she said as she curtsied.

"Good afternoon to you, too, Miss Carrie Emeline."

"Good afternoon to you, also, Mr. Charles."

They entered the dining room and sat at the Wright family table by the window overlooking the courtyard garden. This particular table in the dining room was used for dining by each owner. Christmas Hotel was built in 1850 by Thomas and Lucy Hoy. In 1883 they sold the hotel to Captain Jacob Barnabas Bazell and his wife Mary Eve Winters Bazell who had always eaten each meal in the same location. Before Christopher and Jerilyn married, the Bazells deeded Christmas Hotel to Christopher and Jerilyn as a wedding gift. The Bazells had no living heir. Their daughter Carrie Emeline Bazell had died of pneumonia in 1884.

The hostess informed Jerilyn that today's noon meal special was a cup of cream of broccoli soup with a grilled ham and cheese sandwich. Jerilyn ordered the special for the three of them. While they ate their meal, several of the staff dropped by the table to meet Lucy and say hi to Jerilyn and Carrie Emeline. Lucy expressed a special wish. "I'd like to go to the cabin where Mr. Gabe lives. He's a nice man and I want to thank him."

Jerilyn nodded. "I think that can be arranged, Lucy. Tomorrow is Sunday and we'll attend church, but maybe next Saturday we can do that. On Monday morning, I need to enroll you at Franklin Grade School, which is our local elementary school.

Even though there are only two weeks before Christmas vacation, it's important that you return to your studies as soon as possible. You've already missed one week of school. Carrie Emeline and I will help you get situated and catch up with the other students. Each day after school, you can walk to Christmas Hotel with Carrie Emeline and Ken."

Lucy said nothing.

"What are you thinking, Lucy?"

The child seemed deep in thought. "I won't know anyone. I've attended the elementary school in Bowling Green since kindergarten. What if the other children don't like me?" At that, her face scrunched up, ready to cry.

"I realize it's hard changing schools, Lucy, but with your friendly nature you'll be just fine." Jerilyn patted her hand and Lucy's face radiated, probably at the unexpected compliment, Jerilyn thought.

They finished their meal and walked home. Carrie Emeline and Lucy held hands and skipped all the way. Jerilyn worried that Lucy might get too attached to all of them. She and Christopher needed to discuss Lucy's future – and the sooner the better.

Chapter Seven

Forgiven Sins

"Thou wilt shew me the path of life: in thy presence is fulness of joy; at thy right hand there are pleasures for evermore."
Psalm 16:11

Sunday morning
December 5, 1954
Sunday morning was different today at the Wright home. It had been quite some time since Jerilyn helped a little girl get ready for church. Lily at eighteen and Carrie Emeline at twelve had not required her help for a long time. Jerilyn had laid out Lucy's clothes the night before, and once Lucy was dressed, Jerilyn brushed her hair and added some ribbons. She didn't need to use the hot curling tong on Lucy's hair to create some curls. The girl's hair already had lush curls, unlike her older daughter Lily's hair. Lily's hair was very curly when Jerilyn first met her. However, when Lily was five, she was hit by a car and her head had to be shaved. When her hair grew back in, it was nearly

straight and very fine. Carrie Emeline had waves in her long hair, but her hair could be unruly at times. It was during the unruly times, Carrie Emeline wore her hair in braids or a pony tail.

While Jerilyn brushed her hair, Lucy mentioned, "My mama didn't like brushing my hair in the morning. She always said 'the rats must have slept in it at night,' because it was so tangled in the morning."

"I think that's a 'mama statement,'" Jerilyn replied with a chuckle, but continued to brush. "My mom said that to me when I was a little girl, and I said the same thing to Lily and Carrie Emeline. It helped if I brushed and braided their hair before they went to bed. I'll start doing that with your hair too, if you like."

"Okay," Lucy answered casually. "Last night before Carrie Emeline and I went to sleep, we told stories. She told me that Lily isn't your real daughter, and she and Ken aren't Mr. Christopher's real children. Then she said you're all like a real family and it doesn't make any difference."

Jerilyn smiled at Lucy. "Carrie Emeline is right. My first husband died and I was pregnant with the twins at the time. Lily's mama died giving birth to her. Although tragedy struck all of us, the Lord had a plan for both families. His plan was for Mr. Christopher and me to meet, and me to be his wife and Lily's mama. When the twins were born, Mr. Christopher became their father. We always think of each other as a real family.

"Do you *really* think the Lord has a plan for me, too?"

Jerilyn hugged Lucy. "Yes, I do. He knows your past, present, and future. If you will trust in Him, He will take care of you."

"Do you have any other children?"

Jerilyn struggled with this question. After all these years, it was still painful for her. However, Lucy's question was so honest she wanted to at least answer it partially. "I had two miscarriages, both in the fifth month of pregnancy. Both babies were boys. One happened four years ago and one was two years ago." The third child was too difficult for Jerilyn to talk about. She rarely even discussed that baby with the family. "However, I know I will see those babies again in Heaven," she added. "Do you understand what a miscarriage is?"

"Yes, my Aunt Eula Mae had a miscarriage. She told my mama that the baby would have been born in four more months and that it was a boy, too. My mama said it's a baby that dies in the mama's tummy."

"That's correct. My little boys were perfectly formed little boys that just did not live long enough in my womb to survive in the world." Jerilyn did not add that she blamed herself. She had been stressed about the baby that she declined to speak about.

"Well, young lady, your hair is beautiful and so are you. Let's go make breakfast."

After breakfast, Christopher, Jerilyn, and the three children walked to the church on the square. Christopher preached many Sundays in the chapel at Christmas Hotel, but usually only when the hotel was full of guests. It would be full closer to Christmas.

It was a lovely morning with just a few fluffy clouds in the sky, but the sun was shining. The three children walked ahead of Christopher and Jerilyn, with the twins each holding Lucy's hand as she skipped between them. They met others on the sidewalk and nodded greetings and spoke pleasantries. Pastor Joseph Palmer and his wife Mary met them at the church door. Christopher introduced Lucy before they hung up their coats in the vestibule. The choir sang as the congregation gathered in the sanctuary.

When Pastor Palmer stepped up to the pulpit he asked his congregation to stand for the reading of God's Word. When everyone stood he asked them to turn to Proverbs chapter three, verses five to six, and he read aloud, *"Trust in the Lord with all thine heart; and lean not unto thine own understanding.*

In all thy ways acknowledge him, and he shall direct thy paths."

He then asked the congregation to be seated.

When they left church a little over an hour later, Lucy told Jerilyn that she remembered the verses that the preacher had recited. The pastor at the Methodist Church in Bowling Green had preached this, before her Mama was saved. Lucy said she remembered her mama crying, and at the end of the sermon the pastor had given the usual altar call. Her mama had raised herself from the pew a couple of times, but did not go forward. Finally her mama took her hand and walked out the door. Lucy told Jerilyn that when they arrived home, she had asked her mama, "Why did you cry at church today?" Lucy explained that her mama said, "'I have forgotten how to trust.'"

Christopher suggested they visit Greenlawn Cemetery before heading to Christmas Hotel for the noon meal. "Lucy, we visit here often. It's good to remember those who were a part of our lives." They walked first to the gravesite of Christopher's parents. Christopher explained to Lucy that his own parents had died in a car accident on their wedding anniversary, when he was only four years older than Ken and Carrie Emeline were now.

They next visited the grave of Christopher's first wife, Eleanor "Ellie" Simmons Wright. Christopher turned to Lucy. "Ellie was my first wife, and the mother of my daughter Lily. Ellie died giving birth to Lily."

Jerilyn said, "Lucy, if you recall, I've already told you about Lily's mother. Now you can see where she's buried."

The next grave was of Carrie Emeline Bazell. Lucy turned to Carrie Emeline and said while pointing to the old headstone. "You both have the same name."

"That's correct. Mom found and read this girl's diary. Carrie Emeline *Bazell* lived in the nineteenth century, and her parents owned Christmas Hotel before my parents. While reading the diary, Mom developed a connection with her."

Jerilyn continued the story. "I came to Christmas Hotel quite by accident. I told you my first husband died but not how he died. Kenneth was killed at Pearl Harbor in Hawaii. Have you heard of the attack on Pearl Harbor"

"My mama said it started the war for Americans. She said my daddy was in that war."

"I think there were many Americans in that war before it was over," said Jerilyn. "When my husband was killed, I was only twenty years old and I was in such despair. At the time, I thought it was the worst thing that could happen to me, but the Lord knew better. I wound up at Christmas Hotel where I began to finally heal and have peace."

Jerilyn saw that Lucy appeared to be absorbing all this information. She finally spoke, "Mr. Christopher's parents died when he was very young, and Lily didn't even get to know her mama. Your first husband, who was Ken and Carrie Emeline's daddy, died before they were born. The first Carrie Emeline died young." Lucy lowered her head. "My daddy died before I was born and now I've lost my mama," she said softly. "Life isn't fair, and I can't trust God." She began to cry.

Jerilyn bent down and took Lucy in her arms and held her while she cried. "I know right now it seems that way, and I feel your pain, and I hurt for you. I know it's hard for you to believe, but it will get better. You *must* trust that God will see you through this. We will help you, too. Good things later happened in all our lives, and I sincerely believe good things will happen for you, too."

Lucy just stared at the graves.

Jerilyn stood. "Let me show you this next grave, Lucy. This is Captain and Mrs. Bazell. They were the owners of Christmas Hotel when I first arrived here. They were the parents of the first Carrie Emeline. They moved from Ohio to purchase Christmas Hotel in 1883 when their daughter's fiancé was killed. They helped their daughter in her time of need. If it hadn't been for their kindness, I would probably not be standing here today. The kindness and love the Bazells' showed me definitely helped me through a most difficult time. I learned to trust God again." Jerilyn paused and looked to her right at the last grave they visited. "I'll let Mr. Christopher tell you about this last grave."

Christopher stood quietly at the headstone before he began. "Lydia Grace Evans," he said. "She was like a second mom to me. She was taking care of me when my parents died, and continued to take care of me afterward. She was there for me when my daughter Lily was born and my first wife died. She continued to take care of Lily and me until I met Jerilyn. And then, even after I married Jerilyn, Mrs. Evans was there for all of us. She was there when the twins were born. She was an amazing woman. She died earlier this year. Mrs. Wright and I decided years ago that when we had a daughter we would name her for Mrs. Evans." He stopped abruptly and looked at Jerilyn.

Jerilyn said nothing, but she slipped her hand in his.

Lucy was the first to speak. "Grace is my middle name. Mama said when I was born, she needed grace from God. The name Lucille was already decided by her and my daddy. She said I was her blessing after Daddy died."

"I'm sure you were, Lucy." Jerilyn took Lucy's hand. "Let's all go to Christmas Hotel and have our noon meal."

Chapter Eight

Transitions

"Defend the poor and fatherless: do justice to the
afflicted and needy. Deliver the poor and needy:
rid them out of the hand of the wicked."
Psalm 82:3-4

Monday morning
December 6, 1954
Christopher was already in the dining room when
Jerilyn came down the stairs at five thirty the next
morning. She walked up behind him and put her
arms around him. "You're up early. What're you
doing?" she asked, looking at the pen and paper in
front of him on the table.

He placed his pen on the paper, turned, and
pulled her into his arms so that she sat on his lap.
"I'm writing to the Masonic Widow and Orphan
Home in Louisville. I'm hoping they have room for
Lucy. I didn't tell you, but on Saturday when you
went shopping with the girls, I drove to the Lewis
Memorial Widow and Orphan home on the Bowling
Green Road. They said they were filled at this time.
They still have children not adopted that were
placed there after World War Two and the Korean

War. They suggested I write to Louisville, which is what I'm doing."

Jerilyn tilted her head. "I was planning on enrolling her in the Franklin Grade School this morning. Do you think I should wait until after we hear from Louisville?"

"No. I think Lucy needs to get back to school now. If the Masonic Home does accept Lucy, it may be a couple of weeks, and by then school will be out for Christmas vacation. That will give us time to drive her to Louisville while all our children are out of school. Besides, you've purchased her school clothes and she's excited to go with Ken and Carrie Emeline today. Lucy has had enough disappointments in her short life."

"Yes, she has. I find it disconcerting that so many children have not been adopted. It's been nine years since the Second World War ended, and the Korean War only concluded just over a year ago. If we place Lucy in an orphanage, do you think she'll grow up there?"

"I think this is something we need to pray about. Lucy is in God's hands. I do think she was brought to us for a reason. We need to make sure the Lord's will is fulfilled. I believe it's our first duty."

After breakfast, Christopher left for his work at Christmas Hotel, while Jerilyn walked Lucy to

Franklin Grade School. Ken and Carrie Emeline attended the Franklin-Simpson Junior High. Jerilyn explained Lucy's situation to Principal Timothy Ayers, filled out the required paperwork, and together they walked with Lucy to her third grade classroom.

Principal Ayers called the teacher into the hallway for the introduction. "Mrs. Deaton, this is Lucille Clark and she'll be in your classroom, at least for now." He briefly explained the situation to the teacher and returned to his office.

Jerilyn and Mrs. Deaton exchanged pleasantries. They knew each other, as Mrs. Deaton had been the third grade teacher for the twins. She was unmarried at that time and her name was Miss Jennifer McNamee. She was now married to Steve Deaton, the clerk of courts at the courthouse.

Jerilyn turned to Lucy. "Lucy, remember to wait out front after school, and Ken and Carrie Emeline will pick you up and walk with you to Christmas Hotel. I'm sure you'll be happy in Mrs. Deaton's classroom. Ken and Carrie Emeline enjoyed her as their teacher."

"Thank you, Mrs. Wright," said Mrs. Deaton. "A teacher always likes to know she's appreciated."

Jerilyn bent down and hugged Lucy goodbye. Jerilyn stood, and Mrs. Deaton took Lucy's hand.

As Mrs. Deaton led Lucy toward the classroom,

Mrs. Deaton said to Lucy, "I'll introduce you to the class, Lucy. We're just about to start our reading period and we're reading *Charlotte's Web*. Do you know that book?"

"Yes, I do! We read it at my last school." Lucy said with happiness. She waved to Jerilyn as Mrs. Deaton led her into the classroom. Jerilyn smiled as she left Lucy in secure hands.

Chapter Nine

Uncle Otto and Aunt Eula Mae

*"The wicked plotteth against the just, and
gnasheth upon him with his teeth. The Lord shall
laugh at him: for he seeth that his day is coming."*
Psalm 37: 12-13

*Tuesday morning
December 7, 1954*
Christopher was in the shower when Jerilyn
awakened. She watched as he entered his dressing
room with only his towel around him. She was
sitting at her vanity brushing her hair when he re-
entered their bedroom a few minutes later, now
dressed.

After they said their morning prayers,
Christopher offered a suggestion for the day.
"Jerilyn, I think it's time to visit the apartment
where Lucy lived with her mama. I'd like us to go
alone, after we get the children off to school. Maybe
we can speak with her aunt and uncle and make
certain they really don't want Lucy. We don't want
to send her to an orphanage and later have the aunt
and uncle change their minds."

"I don't know, Christopher. Lucy said they were

mean to her. Are you sure you want to risk turning Lucy over to them?"

"I think we need to see the whole situation for ourselves. If they don't want her, maybe we can at least look at the apartment where she lived with her mama. Possibly we can find something by which Lucy can remember her mama."

"You're right. I'll be ready as soon as the children leave for school."

*****

Christopher and Jerilyn pulled into Bowling Green at 9 am and parked their 1953 Chevrolet Bel Air station wagon in front of *Tandy's Billiards*. Christopher and Jerilyn looked up at the apartment above the billiard parlor and saw a curtain move.

Christopher turned to Jerilyn. "Are you ready?"

"I suppose, but I'm not looking forward to meeting them. Do you think we need to go into the billiard parlor to enter the building?" Jerilyn's brows always knitted together when she was anxious, and now she bit her lower lip too.

"I don't think so, honey. Most of the apartments above a storefront have a rear entrance. Let's go around back and check it out."

When they walked around back, they saw a privy about forty feet from the building, and steps leading up to the apartments. Christopher took Jerilyn's hand. "Let's go."

When they reached the top of the steps, they landed on a small porch and saw the door to enter the building. When they peeked in the door's dirty window, they observed a dark, dingy hallway. Christopher watched Jerilyn's face as she wrinkled her nose in disgust. "The landlord doesn't keep the place very tidy, Christopher."

Christopher laughed. "It's above a billiard parlor, Jerilyn. Did you expect the Taj Mahal?"

The door was unlocked. They opened it and stepped onto the stained floor in the hallway. One dim light bulb hung from the dirty ceiling. There was a door on either side of the hall with #1 and #2 on each door. At the end of the hall steps led down to the lower level.

"Those steps probably lead down to the billiard parlor." Christopher said. "Their apartment must be one of these. I'm going to deduce #2, because I think it has the window where we saw the curtain moving."

They stepped up to the door and Christopher knocked.

They waited and then finally heard footsteps. A disheveled and sloppy obese man in only his pajama bottoms answered the door, but he opened it no more than twelve inches.

"Waddaya want?" the man growled, as he ran his fingers through his long greasy hair, and scratched his hairy belly with the other. His scruffy beard was about four inches in length and streaked with tobacco juice. His breath smelled of sour whiskey. He clearly had been awakened.

"Who's at the door, Otto?" asked a woman in a crotchety voice.

Christopher took Jerilyn's arm protectively. As he was about to make introductions, the woman walked up beside the man, pulling the door open further. Her long stringy hair was uncombed and she wore a dirty robe that she pulled tight around her rotund stomach. Both of them were barefoot.

"We doan want whatever yer sellin!" the woman said to them, also with foul smelling breath. She started to close the door.

"We are not selling anything," said Christopher, using his foot to stop the door from being closed on them. "I am Christopher Wright and this is my wife Jerilyn. We're here in regards to your niece Lucy."

"Well, ya two can go on back ta war ya came from," said the man. "We doan want nuthin' to do with Lucy."

"Please, sir," continued Christopher, "we just want to ask you a few questions. I heard your wife call your name as Otto. May I call you Otto?"

"Sure, why not?" he said sarcastically. "This here's ma wife Eula Mae."

The woman returned a fake smile revealing

misaligned and yellowed teeth. Otto turned and spat toward the spittoon in the apartment, but missed. Tobacco juice ran down the side of the spittoon.

Jerilyn gagged, but Christopher met her eyes for reassurance. "Lucy told my wife and me that her mama died on December first. Is that correct?"

"Yeah, she had the pneumoney," answered Otto. "Rose wuz Eula Mae's sister."

Eula Mae stared at them, displaying no emotion, only a dull expression in her eyes.

Christopher continued, "Lucy told us you did not want her, and asked her to leave your residence. Is that true?"

This time Eula Mae answered. "We got four young 'uns of are own. We doan need 'nother mouth ta feed. If y'all like her so much why doan ya keep her? She ain't wanted here." Eula Mae turned and spat toward the spittoon, and also missed.

Christopher sighed, but made one more attempt to help Lucy. "Was that where Lucy lived with her mama?" he said, as he pointed to the other door.

"Yeah, that's it," answered Otto, clearly disinterested and wanting the questions to be over.

"Do you have a key so we can go in and retrieve some personal items for Lucy?"

"Yeah, I gotta key, but ya won't find much. What was any good wuz took awready. Figgered

Rose owed us fer all them there times we watched after her brat. They's no food, valuables, or money, if that's what ya want."

Christopher was exasperated with them, but he remained calm. "No, sir, we do not. We are hoping to find something that would be sentimental for Lucy to remember her mama. Would you please open the door to their apartment and let us look around?"

Otto shrugged his shoulders and turned back into the apartment. As he swung the door open wider, Christopher and Jerilyn were able to look inside. Not much furniture, just two sagging chairs and two sofas with dirty covers in the front room. One table held a lamp with no shade, along with some dirty dishes and an overflowing ashtray. In the kitchen, dirty dishes were stacked on the counter, the range top, and above the refrigerator. The bare wooden floors were scratched, and the filthy walls looked to have not been painted in some time. Pictures hung haphazardly on two walls. A single light bulb hung from the ceiling, and a foul odor wafted into the hallway.

Otto returned and tossed Christopher the key. "Jus bring it back when yer done," he said brusquely, and slammed the rickety door shut.

Jerilyn spoke softly to Christopher. "I don't want Lucy here with them. We must find her a proper home."

"Don't worry, honey, I won't let Lucy come back here." He turned the key in the lock of apartment #2 and they stepped over the threshold.

At first glance, they could tell the apartment had been ransacked. However, it was not dirty like Otto and Eula Mae's apartment. The walls and floor were clean. White, starched curtains hung in the windows. If any furniture was missing, they could not tell. The scantily furnished living room had two chairs, a sofa and a table. The drawer in the table was open and empty. All the cushions were removed from the chairs and the sofa, and lay on the floor. As they walked into the kitchen, they saw that all the cupboard doors were open, and all the drawers, but it looked like no dishes, towels, or dinnerware were missing. Obviously, whoever ransacked the place was looking only for valuables, or possibly drugs or alcohol.

In the bedroom, the worn but clean bed covers were thrown on the floor, and again the drawers and closet door were open, and rummaged through, but some clothes were still there. The same situation occurred in the bathroom, where the medicine cabinet was open and only a tube of lipstick, a partial bottle of aspirin, a small amount of hydrogen peroxide, two toothbrushes, and tooth powders remained. If there had been anything else, it was now gone. They returned to the bedroom.

On the dresser lay two hair brushes and two combs. Jerilyn searched through the clothing in the closet and in the drawers. "It appears that the best of the clothes have most likely been removed," Jerilyn surmised to Christopher. "Think about Lucy's threadbare coat and the way Lucy was dressed when she arrived at Christmas Hotel. Used clothing was probably the best Rose could afford for her daughter. At least she was clean, though, unlike the Smiths across the hallway."

As they turned to leave, a book caught Christopher's eye. He walked back to the nightstand and in the opened top drawer he picked up a library book, *Time and Time Again* by James Hilton. Below the book lay a Bible. When Christopher opened it he saw that in the front of the Bible was written: *Given to Rose Clark by the Methodist Church on State Street in Bowling Green, Kentucky, Sunday, August 1, 1954 at her baptism.* He handed the Bible to Jerilyn and pointed to what was written.

Jerilyn smiled at Christopher. "This is our memory for Lucy," she said, pressing the Bible to her heart.

They locked the door, walked across the hall, and knocked at Otto and Eula Mae's door. Eula Mae, still in her dingy bathrobe, answered it. Otto was asleep on one of the dirty sofas and snoring, one leg on the sofa's back and the other leg dangling off.

Christopher handed the key to Eula Mae. "We found her mama's Bible. If you don't mind, we would like to give it to Lucy."

"I doan care. She can have it. Good riddance to thet book, an to Rose's brat, too." Eula Mae slammed the wobbly old door.

Christopher and Jerilyn hurried out the back way.

Chapter Ten

Mr. Gabe's Cabin

"And again, I will put my trust in him. And
again, Behold I and the children which God
hath given me."
Hebrews 2:13

Saturday
December 11, 1954
The Saturday on which Christopher and Jerilyn had
agreed to take Lucy to Mr. Gabe's cabin finally
arrived. They all climbed into the station wagon
and drove off, accompanied by Ken, Carrie Emeline
and Bullet. A light snow began to fall, but not
enough to make the road slippery. They turned on
the Bowling Green Road, and Lucy told them that
the cabin was on the right, and closer to Bowling
Green.

Driving along, they came upon a house with an
unusual shape. Lucy pointed to it and said, "I've
seen that house before. What a strange looking
house!"

Christopher, always the historian, smiled and
explained to Lucy that the locals called the house
the Octagon House, because of its eight sides.

"Andrew Jackson Caldwell began construction on the house in 1847 and it took twelve years to complete. His widow lived there until 1918 and sold it to Dr. Miles Williams. Dr. Miles passed away earlier this year. We don't know what will become of this home now." Christopher drove slowly, so Lucy could view the unusual home.

As they drew closer to Mr. Gabe's cabin, Lucy bounced on the seat and pointed. "There's his cabin!" Then her huge smile turned to puzzlement. "That's not the way it looked. I *know* this is the cabin ... but it was *pretty*."

Christopher drove the station wagon onto the gravel road and stopped near the cabin. "Are you *sure* this is the cabin?" he asked. "It looks abandoned."

Lily looked around, staring at the cabin, the barn, and the pasture. There were no cattle grazing in the pasture behind the barn. The shutters on the windows were either askew or had fallen off. The cabin was in dire need of a paint job. The well-maintained flower beds that she previously observed were void of any remembrance of shrubs.

"This *is* the cabin, but *everything* is all wrong." She was clearly perplexed.

The five of them and Bullet stepped out of the car and closed the doors. They walked to the front door that was hanging by one hinge. Christopher pushed the door, being careful that it did not fall off its remaining hinge. The five of them stepped into the cabin, leaving the door open while Bullet ran around back. Dust and cobwebs covered the cabin.

"Watch where you walk," warned Christopher, while wiping cobwebs from his face. "Some of the floorboards are missing."

Lucy pointed in the room. "Those two rocking chairs were just like that in front of the fireplace, but that's not the way they looked before. They've got dust and cobwebs all over them, and one has a missing arm and a missing rocker and the other has two missing slats," Lucy observed. She looked above the fireplace. "That picture of the woman was there, but now it's all faded and the frame is broken. All those pictures scattered in the corner were hanging on the walls right here." She pointed to the walls where the pictures had hung.

She ran to the kitchen. "Mr. Gabe cooked us breakfast on that stove," she said as she pointed to the rusted old iron wood stove. "When I was here with Mr. Gabe, there was wood stacked beside the stove. We ate at the table." The oak table now leaned with one of its legs broken and there was only one broken chair remaining. The ice box and the pie safe were gone. She described to them how the kitchen looked when she was there before.

Lucy ran to the bedroom in which she had slept.

There were no frilly curtains at the now cracked and grimy windows. The bed was broken with no pretty quilts and pillows. The rocking chair was gone. There was no braided rug covering a beautiful, and highly polished wood floor. The floor was in need of repair and there was even a big hole in the wall under the window.

Lucy began to cry. Jerilyn knelt and held her, trying to soothe the little girl.

"Where is Mr. Gabe? What happened? I don't understand." Her body shook and she choked out her words.

Bullet ran in from the open front door and rushed to Lucy. He lay on the floor whimpering beside her.

Lucy withdrew from Jerilyn's embrace and flung her little body on Bullet, burying her face into his fur and placing her arms around him.

Jerilyn stood and looked up at Christopher. He merely shook his head in answer to her silent question. Ken frowned and Carrie Emeline bit her lip.

Christopher bent down to Lucy. "Let's go home," he said softly. He held out his hand and she took it.

The family, with Bullet trailing, walked back to the car, lost in their own thoughts.

Chapter Eleven

The Visitors

*"He coveteth greedily all the day long: but the
righteous giveth and spareth not."*
Proverbs 21:26

Monday
December 13, 1954
An old rusted out jalopy pulled up to the curb in
front of Christmas Hotel. The engine sputtered and
coughed, and it finally died. A couple climbed from
the car and slammed the shaky doors. They hurried
to the double brass doors, opened one, and
marched in.

"Whewee!" exclaimed the woman, moving her
long, stringy, dirty hair from her face and tucking it
behind her ears. "These are *some* digs!"

The two swaggered up to the Christmas tree,
completely ignoring Christopher and Jerilyn who
were sitting behind the desk.

Otto touched the tree. "It ain't real, Eula Mae.
I'd wager those boxes under it ar fake, too. These
people ain't as rich as they put on."

Eula Mae swept the room with her red, watery
eyes. "I dunno, Otto. Lookit that staircase. I'd bet

my last dollar it's solid cherry. Lookit all them decorations in this here room," she said, while reaching inside her shirt, adjusting her brassiere strap, and removing a handkerchief from the brassiere. She blew her nose loudly and stuffed the handkerchief back. Her too small tattered coat lay open with no buttons. She wore what resembled men's work trousers. Otto wore no coat, just two shirts and a pair of coveralls with holes in the knees, along with an old and worn floppy hat.

They turned and pretended to notice Christopher and Jerilyn for the first time.

"Lookee here, Otto. Them's the Wrights all dolled up in Christmas clothes."

Christopher walked from behind the desk. "May I help you?" he inquired in a stern voice, but did not shake their hands.

"We jus wanted ta see whar our sweet lil Lucy was livin'," answered Eula Mae. "We heared you owned a hotel, an we needed to make certain it weren't trashy. Only the best fur ar li'l Lucy."

"That's right," piped in Otto. "We cain't have that sweet young 'un in a fleabag flophouse. We's just watchin' out fur her, ya understand ... right?" he said, as he addressed Christopher. He then turned to Jerilyn, nodded his head without removing his hat and said with his best fake smile, "Afternoon, ma'am."

"You did not seem concerned when we were at your apartment last week," Christopher said in a strict voice. "Why are you really here?"

"Like we said," responded Eula Mae in a sugary sweet tone, "we need ta make sure ar Lucy is farin' okay."

This time Jerilyn spoke from behind the desk. "Lucy is just fine and she's presently at school. If you would like a periodic update on her, I'm sure Mr. Wright and I can mail you a monthly report."

A young married couple who checked in yesterday descended the staircase. They looked from Christopher and Jerilyn to the unknown couple, obviously realized they were in the middle of a confrontation, and hurried out the front door.

"We doan want no report," Otto responded in a more severe voice than Christopher. "We want ar Lucy back."

Christopher heard Jerilyn's gasp and he addressed Otto. "You can't be serious! You already have four children you can't support. This is the first I've heard you say you want to care for Lucy. I'm going to ask you one more time ... what's the real reason?" He was now angry. Jerilyn moved from behind the desk to stand beside her husband.

"She belongs to us," answered Eula Mae. "She's ar kin. Otto an I will jus wait in this here lobby 'til she comes in from school." She moved toward the chairs by the tree.

"Wait, Eula Mae," Otto said. "It 'pears the Wrights ain't right takin' with us raisin' Lucy," he said as he scratched his scruffy, tobacco stained beard. "Maybe they'd like ta make us an offer so's they can keep her."

"Now, I see exactly what you really want," said Christopher, eyes blazing. "You two came here to try and sell your rights to Lucy. Well, I'm letting you know it's not going to work. I will make sure you don't get your hands on her. I don't know who will be raising Lucy, but it won't be the likes of you two. Now get out of here!" He said in a loud and angry voice, while striding toward the door to escort them out.

"We ain't budgin'!" Otto shouted. "Come on, Eula Mae; let's have a seat on that fancy sofa." He grabbed her arm to pull her to the sofa.

At that second, Bullet came from around the desk where he had been napping. He stood in front of Otto and Eula Mae and snarled viciously, showing all his teeth, and poised to leap.

"Call off yer dog!" yelled Otto, as he jumped back. Eula Mae scurried to hide behind her husband.

Christopher walked to Bullet and petted him. "It's okay, Bullet. Lie down."

Bullet obeyed, but kept his eyes on Otto and

Eula Mae; a low, throaty growl still persisted in warning.

"We'll leave, but mind you this ain't settled. We'll be back," Otto said, but not as loud as he had been. He and Eula Mae kept their eyes on Bullet and backed slowly toward the door.

Christopher and Jerilyn opened the door, and Otto and Eula Mae left the hotel. They watched Otto and Eula Mae get in the old car and slam the doors. After three attempts, the engine finally started with a backfire. The bald tires screeched as they sped off.

Jerilyn looked up at Christopher. "What can we do? We can't give Lucy back to them."

"I'm not sure, honey. The court might say they are the next of kin and award her to them. Maybe we should go to Judge James, Jr. and plead for temporary custody until the orphanage in Louisville has an opening. I fear we have not seen the last of Otto and Eula Mae."

*****

That evening, Jerilyn entered the bedroom that Carrie Emeline now shared with Lucy. Carrie Emeline was in the bubble bath, and Lucy sat cross-legged on the floor reading from the book of Genesis in her mama's Bible while absentmindedly petting Bullet. Lucy was overcome with joy last week when Christopher and Jerilyn presented her with this treasured possession belonging to her mama. Lucy turned her head, laid down the book, and smiled as Jerilyn entered the room. Jerilyn walked over, bent down and petted Bullet. Lucy had finished her bath and was wearing one of Carrie Emeline's clean nightgowns.

Jerilyn took Lucy's hand. "Come over to the vanity and let me brush your hair and braid it."

Jerilyn picked up the brush and began brushing the curly locks. "Would you tell me about the night your mama died, and more about your aunt and uncle? Did you run away?"

Lucy expelled a sigh of despair. With sad eyes, she looked at Jerilyn in the mirror. Finally she said, "Mama had been sick for a long time. She kept coughing and couldn't go to work. She told me the night before she died that she needed to go to the hospital, but she'd wait until morning. Mama hadn't been out of bed for two days. She said she needed to take care of some things before she went to the hospital. She told me how much she loved me and no matter what happened to her, she wanted me to forgive her.

"I didn't understand why she wanted me to forgive her, and I still don't. I told her I loved her, too, and I had nothing to forgive her for. She told me that someday I'd understand. She asked me to bring her the writing paper and a pen, so she could write something. She had some paper in the drawer in our living room and I took it to her with a pen. She asked me to go back in the living room while she wrote. That's what I did, and then I fell asleep on the sofa.

"The next morning I woke up on the sofa, when the sun came up. I fixed myself a piece of toast and a glass of milk, and then I went into the bedroom to see if I could bring my mama something to eat. She was still in bed and I thought she was asleep."

A tear trickled from Lucy's eye. Carrie Emeline walked into the bedroom and stopped. She quietly closed the door and sat on her bed.

"I touched my mama and she was cold. I tried to shake her, but it was no use. I knew something was wrong and I ran to get Uncle Otto and Aunt Eula Mae. I told them Mama was not waking up. They walked across the hall with my four cousins. My cousins sat down on the sofa and the two chairs. There was no room for me, so I sat in the corner on the floor, with my knees up to my chest. Uncle Otto and Aunt Eula Mae went into the bedroom. When they came out they just said my mama was dead. My cousins kept calling me 'little orphan girl' and laughed at me. They all walked out and left me on the floor in the corner."

At that, Jerilyn knelt beside Lucy and took her in her arms. Lucy cried as she relived what happened. When Lucy finished crying, Jerilyn handed her a handkerchief.

Lucy continued, although her voice was now hoarse. "Later, I did go back into the bedroom and lay on the bed beside my mama. I knew she was no longer alive, but I tried to hold on to her. I was scared. Sometime later, my aunt and uncle came back and told me I had to get out. They said I was nothing but garbage, and they didn't want me. They began opening drawers and doors. Aunt Eula Mae took some of Mama's clothes, while Uncle Otto searched through the rest of what was in the drawers. I put on my coat and left. I didn't run away. They *made* me leave." Lucy began to cry again.

Jerilyn pulled Lucy onto her lap and rocked her, talking to her soothingly. She looked over at Carrie Emeline who sat on the bed with her face in her hands.

"Why did my mama have to die?" Lucy lamented. "I miss her so much. Why do my aunt and uncle hate me? I tried so hard to be a good girl for them."

"I don't know the answer to any of your questions, honey. I know it's hard to lose someone, but I do know it will get easier to bear. Please know I understand your pain. God knows your pain. As far as your aunt and uncle, God will have to deal with them. What they did to you is wrong, very wrong."

"What will happen to me, Miss Jerilyn? If they don't want me, where will I go? I don't have other family."

"I don't know, honey, but Mr. Christopher and I are working on this. Please don't worry. In the meantime, try to get some sleep. Let's say prayers and then I'll tuck you in."

Bullet followed Lucy to the bed and lay on the floor beside her. Both girls knelt on the floor by their beds and Jerilyn knelt between them. She heard their prayers and then she prayed for each one. Jerilyn hugged them and tucked them in.

"I wish both of you sweet dreams," Jerilyn said to each girl, and kissed them on their foreheads. She turned out the light and closed the door.

Dear God, help us help Lucy, Jerilyn prayed in her heart as she leaned on the closed door outside the room.

Chapter Twelve

The Sheriff

*"And be ye kind one to another, tenderhearted,
forgiving one another, even as God for Christ's
sake hath forgiven you."*
Ephesians 4:32

Thursday morning
December 16, 1954
At 9 am, just after the three children began their
walk to school, there was a knock on the front door
of the Wright residence. "Good morning, Sheriff
Scott," said Christopher when he opened the door.
Jerilyn walked up behind him.

"Mr. Wright, I'm here on official business. I
apologize, but I need to ask if you are harboring an
eight-year-old girl named Lucille Grace Clark?"

Christopher paused, staring into the sheriff's
eyes, and then he swung the door wide open and
said, "Please come in, Sheriff. I think we need to
talk."

After they were seated, Jerilyn joined them with
a pot of coffee and three cups. While she poured,
Christopher began the story of how Lucy and a dog
were brought to them on December third by an old

man, who they only knew as Mr. Gabe. Bullet took that moment to enter the room and lay in front of the fireplace beside Daisy. Christopher relayed to the sheriff about their two encounters with the aunt and uncle. He informed him of his efforts to get Lucy into the Lewis Memorial Widow and Orphan home to no avail. He explained he was currently waiting on a response to his letter at the Masonic Widow and Orphan Home in Louisville.

"You see, Sheriff, the aunt and uncle did not want Lucy until they thought they might gain financially by acquiring her from us. They thought we would actually pay them for her. I want that little girl to have a chance at a good home. I believe that's why Mr. Gabe brought her to us."

The sheriff set his cup in the saucer and rubbed his temple. This time he addressed them informally. Darius Scott and Christopher were actually old school friends. "Christopher, I regret what I'm about to tell you and Jerilyn. I have a court order to return a Miss Lucille Grace Clark to her next of kin Otto and Eula Mae Smith, to their residence in Bowling Green, Kentucky."

Jerilyn gasped when she heard the news. Christopher picked up her hand to comfort her as much as him. "When do you have to take her, Darius?" Christopher asked, as calmly as possible.

"I have four days. I would need to pick her up

on Monday morning. I'm sorry, but I have no choice. I'm especially sorry after the stories you told me about the aunt and uncle, but it's the law."

"We understand your obligation, Darius," said Christopher. "We don't fault you."

After the sheriff left, Christopher called his assistant manager at Christmas Hotel, letting him know they would not be in before Monday. He sat back down on the sofa with Jerilyn. "How and when do we tell her, Christopher?" asked Jerilyn.

"The first thing we need to do is see Judge James. We need to try and stop this court order. If we're successful, we'll just wait until we hear from the orphanage in Louisville. If we aren't successful, I say we wait until Sunday night. Lily will be home from the University of Kentucky tomorrow. Let's have an enjoyable time with all four children Saturday. We can go see that movie *White Christmas* all of you want to see, and attend church as always on Sunday. I want to preach in the chapel at Christmas Hotel this Sunday. The Lord has given me a message, and I feel like it needs to be preached this Sunday and not next."

"I pray Judge James sides with us, Christopher. I can't imagine Lucy living with her aunt and uncle. I know they don't want her. I just feel Lucy was brought here for us to help her."

Jerilyn sat back on the sofa and rested her head

against its back. She closed her eyes, and with a big sigh said, "Christopher, do you ever wonder about Lydia Grace?" She opened her teary eyes and he searched them. "Ever since Lucy arrived, I've been thinking about her. I can't help it. They're only twenty-four days apart in age. I wonder what our Lydia Grace is like. I know we don't normally speak of her, but I feel I need to now. Do you think about her much?"

Christopher stared deeply into Jerilyn's eyes. He also sighed and hung his head. After a moment he looked back at Jerilyn and took her hand. "I think about her a great deal. I've spent the past eight years wondering if I should bring up her name to you. I've wanted to talk about her. The twins hardly remember her. They were only four and a half, but Lily certainly does. She won't discuss Lydia Grace with you, because she knows how much pain it causes you. She does talk with me about her, though."

"I didn't know that," Jerilyn said softly. "What does Lily say to you?"

"She says things like 'I wonder if her hair is still curly and brown.' She says she hopes so, because she had curly brown hair before the automobile hit her, and the nurses shaved her head. She asks me if I think she has brown eyes like she and I have, or maybe blue like your eyes and the twins. She always asks to pray with me, hoping the person who stole Lydia Grace from us is taking good care of her. She asks that we pray for the nursing staff at Protestant Hospital in Nashville, because they probably still blame themselves for the kidnapping."

"I'm sorry, Christopher, that I haven't been there for you and Lily." A tear trickled down Jerilyn's cheek and she quickly wiped it away. "I've been so selfish. I knew you were suffering and in pain, too, but I just didn't want to deal with it. I know it was the stress of holding in the pain that caused the miscarriages of each of our two sons. Christopher, I'm so sorry. I should have discussed Lydia Grace with you much more than I did. Please ... forgive me," She choked out and began to cry. Her shoulders were shaking when Christopher took her in his arms, and together they cried.

"We need to talk to Lily while she's home," said Jerilyn, trying to control her unsteady voice. "It's good for her to remember Lydia Grace, the baby sister she never knew. We should talk about her with the twins, too."

"I feel like I've finally gotten my wife back. I love you, Jerilyn."

"I love you, too, Christopher. Now let's go see Judge James to see what we can do to help Lucy."

*****

Four hours later they returned home with no resolution. The judge did see them, showed compassion for the situation, but said there really was nothing he could do. The Smiths were the next of kin, and if they wanted Lucy they were now the legal guardians. The law could not step in unless child abuse or negligence became a factor, and being uneducated and poor certainly did not count as a crime.

Christopher and Jerilyn vowed to make this a happy weekend for Lucy. They prayed together for Lucy's welfare.

Chapter Thirteen

Homecoming for Lily

"Casting all your care upon him; for he careth for you."
1 Peter 5:7

Friday afternoon
December 17, 1954
Christopher and Jerilyn ran down the front steps to the car in which their older daughter Lily arrived. Lily jumped out, hugged and kissed her parents, and introduced the two girls she was with as her new friends at the University of Kentucky: Jill Sanders and Grecia Vaughn. She had written to her parents early in December that her dormitory roommates, who lived in nearby Scottsville, would bring her home. Therefore, Christopher and Jerilyn would not need to drive to Lexington and pick her up.

Jill stepped from the driver's seat, opened the trunk, and handed Christopher Lily's suitcase. Lily thanked her school chums and waved goodbye. The two promised to pick up Lily early on January second when they returned to school.

Lily had barely gotten in the door, when she

nonchalantly asked, "So what's new?"

The three younger children were due to arrive home soon, so Christopher and Jerilyn knew they did not have much time to explain Lucy.

"Have a seat, honey. We have a story to tell you, but first I'll just take your suitcase up to your room."

When Christopher returned a couple of minutes later, Jerilyn and Lily were sitting on the sofa chatting away, with their old dog Daisy lying placidly at their feet. "I was accepted on the cheerleading team," Lily said excitedly. "I've already cheered for many of the football games. I'm trying out for lead cheerleader, so you'll have to teach me some of the moves from when you were a cheerleader!"

"That seems like ages ago," said Jerilyn. "I was only a junior high and high school cheerleader, since I didn't go to college. You've cheered for junior high, high school, and now college. You'll have to show Carrie Emeline some cheers. She just made the junior high team."

"Am I interrupting my girls?" asked Christopher, as he took a seat across from them.

"Oh, Daddy, of course not," Lily said smiling. "I love school, but I'm so happy to be home. Okay, what are you two going to tell me that's new and exciting?"

"We're going to have to be quick because Ken, Carrie Emeline ... and Lucy will be home from school in about thirty minutes," said Christopher.

"Lucy?" Lily lifted one eyebrow. "Who's Lucy?"

"That's a long story," said Christopher, "but we'll give you the abbreviated version."

He and Jerilyn went through all the events from December first until the present. Lily listened in sadness about the death of Lucy's mama, and in horror about the aunt and uncle. When they finished, she asked, "Can they really make Lucy return to that ghastly family?"

"It seems so," said Jerilyn. "Your father and I went to see Judge James yesterday, and he was sympathetic, but said it was the law. The aunt and uncle are the next of kin. If the aunt and uncle really want Lucy, they can take her, by law."

"I don't understand," responded Lily, clearly perplexed. "When the aunt and uncle were at Christmas Hotel, they said they wanted money. Did you tell Judge James what they said?"

"We did," said Jerilyn. "We can't prove anything. There were no witnesses to the situation. Therefore, even though Judge James believes us, it wouldn't stand up in a court of law."

Before Lily could ask another question, Bullet trotted into the room wagging his tail, knowing it was about time for Lucy to come home.

"Whoa! That's one big dog!"

Christopher and Jerilyn laughed as Bullet sauntered up to Lily and greeted her by licking her hand with his huge tongue while wagging his long tail.

"I think he likes you," said Christopher laughing.

Lily hesitantly petted him gently on the head. She was accustomed to Daisy who had been a part of their family for fifteen years, but Daisy only weighed about thirty pounds. Bullet was at least a hundred pounds, and probably much more. He placed his big paws on her lap, and she scratched him behind the ears.

"So Bullet is Lucy's bodyguard. I'd hate to see what would happen to the person that would hurt her." She looked at her dad and asked with concern, "Will Bullet be able to live with Lucy at the aunt and uncle's apartment?"

"That's a good question. I suppose we won't know until the sheriff takes them both Monday morning."

The conversation was interrupted when the front door burst open. The three children rushed into the living room, and Ken and Carrie Emeline hurried to embrace Lily as soon as they saw her. Lucy stood hesitantly on the threshold of the living room shuffling her feet from side to side. Bullet ran to Lucy and she bent down and hugged him.

Jerilyn stood. "Lucy, please come in and meet Lily."

Lily stood as introductions were made and then she hugged Lucy. "It's nice to meet you, Lucy."

"It's nice to meet you, too, Lily," Lucy said, returning the hug.

Lily said, "I suppose you three are glad school is out for Christmas break." They nodded. "I know I am. I'm ready to do some fun, family things. On the way home, I saw that *White Christmas* is showing at the Roxy Theater. Do you think we can all go tomorrow?" she asked as she looked at her parents.

"Your father and I had already planned the movie for us," said Jerilyn. "We can all have the noon meal at Christmas Hotel and then go to the two pm showing. How does that sound?"

"Wonderful!" all the children chorused.

Chapter Fourteen

Family Time

*"And let the peace of God rule in your hearts, to
the which also ye are called in one body; and be
ye thankful."*
Colossians 3:15

Saturday
December 18, 1954
The next morning the house was noisy with four
children around the breakfast table. The three
Wright children laughed, joked, and generally
caught up with each other's lives and did their best
to make Lucy feel welcome. Jerilyn and Christopher
listened to the children's conversations while
cooking. Saturday morning breakfast was always a
wonderful family experience for the Wrights.
During the weekdays, they generally ate a quick
breakfast and then headed to their duties at
Christmas Hotel and the children left for school.
They did not have time for a feast, but on Saturday
morning they did. Birthdays and holidays
warranted extra preparation, and now
homecomings were added to the list.

Steaming platters of Lily's favorite breakfast:

blueberry pancakes, scrambled eggs, link sausage, were placed across the center of the table. The family joined hands and Christopher asked the blessing.

The children were excited, not only because Lily was home, but also because in the afternoon they were going to see *White Christmas* at the Roxy. A heavy snow continued to fall, and so playing in the snow was also on the day's agenda, immediately following breakfast. Christopher promised to help them build igloos, and with all the snow, the girls planned to build two snowmen.

With breakfast finished, Jerilyn begged off building igloos and snowmen and chose to clean up the kitchen, so Christopher headed out back with the four bundled children and both dogs. Daisy acted like a pup, as she playfully chased Bullet around the back yard, nipping at his hind legs.

Christopher and Ken each grabbed snow shovels and began to make three piles with long mounds of snow between the three piles. The three girls rolled small balls of snow into bigger balls of snow to stack them together for the snowmen. Christopher and Ken pounded down the snow heaps and then dug out a hole in the front of the three mounds and used their bodies to burrow the tunnel passages between the three igloos. Lucy watched and laughed. She said she had never seen an igloo built, nor had she ever built a snowman. When they were finished, they poured water over the snow to form ice. While the guys finished the igloo, the three girls decorated the two snowmen with scarves, top hats, buttons for the noses, and coal for the eyes.

"The snowmen look like the song by Gene Autry!" said Lucy. "We just need some corncob pipes!"

"I know where we can get some," said Lily, with a wink and a twinkle in her eye. "Mr. Davidson, our butcher who lives over on Morris Street, smokes pipes. He'll loan them to us. Is it okay if we ask him, Daddy?"

"It's fine by me," said Christopher. "You girls go ahead. Maybe we can get your mom out here in the meantime."

By the time the girls returned with the pipes, Christopher and Ken, along with Jerilyn, were snuggled up in the igloos. The three girls put the pipes in the two snowmen's mouths and joined the others in the igloos. They had made the igloos really large this year so all six of them would fit inside, along with the two dogs. Daisy and Bullet weren't certain what to do. They paced back and forth before finally deciding to enter.

"It's really warm in here," said Lucy. "I've never been in an igloo before."

"Daddy and I have been building igloos since I was a little girl," said Lily. "We didn't get Mom in an igloo the first year Daddy and I met her, because she was pregnant with Ken and Carrie Emeline. The following winter, when Ken and Carrie Emeline were still babies, we *all* were out here in the igloos. It's one of our family traditions." She turned to Lucy. "Did you and your mama have family traditions?"

"When Mama wasn't working, we did things like walk to the fountain in Bowling Green. It's just as pretty in the winter as it is in the summer. I like watching the snow hit the water, and when it rains, it makes little ripples in the water. Mama brought me to Christmas Hotel when she said we had some extra money. I never came at Christmas time, but it didn't matter, since every day is Christmas at Christmas Hotel. We went to the Bowling Green library a lot. Mama let me pick out any book I wanted. Sometimes we would just sit at the library and read. Mama called it the best free entertainment ever. I really enjoyed the *Caddie Woodlawn* stories, and I read all those books. We went to movies at the State Theater on Saturday when Mama wasn't working. We also went to church ... sometimes, but more often after Mama got saved. I still don't understand what she was saved from. Do those count as family traditions?"

she asked.

Lily touched Lucy's arm in the dim light of the igloo, and smiled. "Yes, Lucy, they definitely count. Those are good memories, and you make sure you hang on to them and don't forget, because they belong only to you."

Lucy hugged Lily. "I won't forget. Thank you, Lily."

"Well, family," said Jerilyn, "we need to get cleaned up for our noon meal and the movie. Let's crawl out of the igloos."

"Yay, for the movie!" they all yelled.

*****

When the movie ended and the theater let out, the audience burst out onto South Main Street. Some were singing, some were crying, and most of the women were doing both. The women of the Wright family and Lucy were in the latter group, while Christopher and Ken just joined the crowd in song. A steady snow was still falling, and there already appeared to be about six inches on the ground. There were no cars on the streets, and everyone was on foot.

"I'm Dreaming of a White Christmas," they sang.

Across the street a man was shoveling his steps. "I think you're getting it!" he yelled, but not so good-naturedly. The family just laughed as they continued to sing on their walk home.

"What was your favorite part, Mom?" asked Carrie Emeline.

"Well, I'm a bit of a romantic. I like the part when Rosemary Clooney realized she was wrong about Bing Crosby. I liked their making up," Jerilyn said, as she snuggled closer into Christopher, taking his arm.

"I liked the opening when the battle occurred and Danny Kaye saved his commanding officer's life," said Ken.

"That was my favorite part, too, Ken," Christopher agreed.

"You men just like action," said Lily. "We women like the tender parts. I liked the scene when Danny Kaye and Vera-Ellen danced. That was so lovely and romantic."

"I liked that scene, too," agreed Carrie Emeline. Then she addressed Lucy. "What was your favorite part, Lucy?"

"I liked it all, but especially the ending. When all those men that served in the war under General Waverly came back to let him know how much they cared for him, I cried. It's nice to have people care about you and love you."

Carrie Emeline placed her arm around Lucy as the family continued the walk home.

By the time they returned home, the snow had

begun to subside, so Christopher and Jerilyn suggested they drive out to the McLemore farm, cut down the tree, bring it home, and trim it. Everyone piled into the station wagon, along with Bullet, and driving very slowly they were off to Nettie Sue and Booker's farm. Just one week earlier, Christopher had spent the day putting chains on the tires to ensure as much traction in the snow as possible.

Along the way to the farm, Christopher explained to Lucy their Christmas tree tradition. "Lucy, each year we drive to the McLemore's family farm, cut down the tree, take lots of pictures, and decorate the tree on the same evening. In the past, we've set aside the first Saturday in December for the event, which this year was December fourth and two weeks ago. However, we knew we could not do this without Lily, especially when trimming the tree is her favorite time at Christmas. Therefore, we all agreed to wait until Lily arrived home from school. While Lily's in college, that will become our new tradition."

Nettie Sue and Booker lived on her daddy's farm twelve miles out in the country. Her dad Roy Harris was deceased, but her mother Josie Harris lived with them. Jerilyn met Nettie Sue when she first arrived in Franklin back in December, 1941. Nettie Sue and Booker married when he returned from the war. Jerilyn and Nettie Sue were now life-long friends.

The McLemores ate the noon meal at Christmas Hotel most Saturdays when they drove into town for supplies. Jerilyn and Christopher spent at least one Sunday each month after church at the McLemore farm savoring Nettie Sue's southern fried chicken, home grown vegetables, fruit pies, and cornbread. She baked the best pies made from the pecan, cherry, apple, and peach trees that she nurtured in her orchard. Every fall, Nettie Sue canned her own fruit and vegetables, like a typical farmer's wife.

It had been a tradition for both families to cut down their cedar Christmas tree together each year. Knowing that Lily was away at school, Nettie Sue, Booker and their two little boys six-year-old Jimmy and three-year-old Robert, also waited to cut down their tree this year.

When the Wrights pulled into the long gravel driveway, the family dog ran toward them and barked. He stopped barking and wagged his tail when he saw it was the familiar Wright family. Several of their many barn cats darted across the driveway. The Wrights opened the car doors, and the family along with Bullet emerged. The two dogs sniffed each other and then began to play in the snow. The McLemores opened the front door.

"Come on in!" Lucy was introduced. The day before, Jerilyn had called Nettie Sue and explained Lucy's situation. Nettie Sue hugged Lucy. "It's a pleasure to meet you, Lucy."

Ever polite, Lucy returned the hug. "Thank you, ma'am, and it's a pleasure to meet all of you, too."

Mama Harris called everyone into the kitchen. "Take off your coats. You need to warm up with hot cocoa and a slice of my hot apple pie before you head to the tree area."

Christopher had ordered the latest Leica camera a few months earlier, and it arrived two weeks ago. He brought the camera with him to record their tree cutting expedition, and he snapped several pictures in the home with Mama Harris serving the cocoa, the children drinking the cocoa, and capturing the brown mustaches on Robert's, Jimmy's, and Lucy's upper lips.

Earlier, before the Wrights arrived, Booker had hooked up the wagon to the tractor. Three adults and six children piled in the wagon and wrapped the horsehair blankets around themselves, while Booker climbed up behind the wheel of the tractor. This was a new experience for Lucy, who giggled with delight.

"What Christmas songs do you want to sing?" Jerilyn asked.

"O Little Town of Bethlehem," answered Lily.

Carrie Emeline laughed, and explained to Lucy, "That's Lily's favorite hymn. We don't begin *any* event without first singing 'O Little Town of Bethlehem.' But it's okay with Ken and me. It wouldn't be Christmas without Lily home."

The ten voices rang out across the fields. They sang "Joy to the World" next, while Booker drove them down the gravel driveway and across the road to their other farm with the two dogs running beside them.

When they reached the thicket of cedar trees, Booker shut off the tractor's engine and everyone climbed down. Christopher photographed the six children while they examined every tree until they chose their two favorites. Booker grabbed his two handsaws, and he and Ken cut down the two chosen trees, tossed them in the wagon, while Christopher continued to snap pictures. Everyone climbed in and Booker drove them back across the road with the dogs barking excitedly, and running alongside the wagon. The family and friends sang more Christmas hymns as they bounced along in the wagon on the bumpy road.

Christopher and Ken tied their tree to the top of the station wagon. Shaking Booker's hand, Christopher thanked him. "It's been our pleasure, as always," responded Booker, and Jerilyn and Nettie Sue hugged.

Lily, Carrie Emeline, and Ken waved and added, "Merry Christmas!"

The sun had set by the time they arrived home. Ruth, who was Lily's best friend since childhood, ran across the street with Bonnie her Collie at her heels. Lily jumped out of the car to hug her friend and Bullet began to bark. Ruth was alarmed, and with big eyes and some apprehension, she asked, "Is ... he friendly?"

Lily laughed and said, "Yes, he's friendly. I had the same reaction when I first saw him yesterday." Ken opened the tailgate and Bullet jumped out and ran to Bonnie. "It looks as though Bullet is making another friend." Lily laughed. "He'll soon have more friends than I have!"

Ruth watched as Lucy emerged. Ruth attended her first semester of college in Bowling Green, Kentucky at Western Kentucky University.

"I didn't get home from Western until today," she explained. Then she whispered to Lily, "Mama told me about Lucy. How sad that Lucy's mama died on her birthday."

"Yes, it is," agreed Lily. "My parents have been trying to help her get in to one of the orphanages either here or Louisville. Our local orphanage was full and my parents haven't heard from the one in Louisville, but it won't matter. Her aunt and uncle have decided they want her. They're a couple of repugnant individuals and certainly shouldn't have custody of Lucy or their own four children, but that's another story. Come on in and help us decorate the tree and sing Christmas carols. Bonnie can come in, too."

Christopher and Ken untied the tree and carried it into the house while Carrie Emeline held the door open. Lily, Ruth, Jerilyn, and Lucy hurried to the basement to get the stand, and carried up the boxes of decorations. Daisy rested her tired old bones on the warm hearth, while Bullet and Bonnie roughhoused.

Jerilyn let the big dogs out in the back yard before they destroyed her living room.

Christopher held the tree erect, while Ken screwed the bolts into the tree. "Yay, the tree's straight!" yelled Carrie Emeline, while putting a stack of 78 RPM singles of Christmas songs on the record player.

Lily and Ruth were in charge of the lights, and they wound the strings of bubble lights on the tree and the twinkle lights around the windows. They decorated the stairwell and the upstairs outside balcony with strings of holly and lights. They finished with the outside lights, wrapping them around the columns in front of the house. As soon as Lily and Ruth had finished the lights on the tree, the others each grabbed a box of ornaments and sang along to the Christmas records. They finished with tinsel and garland, then stood back to admire their handiwork.

"It's the best tree ever!" declared Lily.

"You say that every year," said Ken.

"Well, this year we had Lucy helping," she said, and hugged the child to her side.

Lucy looked up at Lily and beamed her appreciation. "My mama and I decorated a tree every year, but it wasn't as grand as this one. We only had the space for a small tree on the tabletop. Mama didn't own a record player to play Christmas songs, but we did listen to the carolers walk the street, singing Christmas songs."

"We'll be doing that on Christmas Eve—" Carrie Emeline began and stopped herself. She turned and whispered to Ken, "Lucy will be back with her aunt and uncle on Christmas Eve. I almost told Lucy she would be singing carols with us."

"We all should be more careful what we say around Lucy," Ken whispered back.

Lily ran upstairs and brought down some wrapped parcels, placing them under the tree. "The tree looks so bare, I thought I'd put the presents around it that I purchased in Lexington."

Ken started to kneel under the tree and check them out. Lily put a hand on his arm, "Not so fast, little brother. I know how you are. You just want to shake the package with your name on it and guess what's inside."

"Of course, big sis. That's half the fun, isn't it?"

"Do you think you can at least wait until Christmas?"

"I'll try," he said, poking her gently in the ribs with his elbow, "but I can't promise."

Lucy stood back and watched the family as they teased, laughed, joked, and sang. *I want to live in a family like this family.*

Chapter Fifteen

The Sermon

"Peace I leave with you, my peace I give unto you: not as the world giveth, give I unto you. Let not your heart be troubled, neither let it be afraid."
John 14:27

Sunday morning
December 19, 1954
The Wright family left their home early Sunday morning to walk to Christmas Hotel. Christopher would be preaching that morning, and with the hotel full to capacity, he expected the little chapel in the hotel would be packed, with people spilled into the lobby. That was fine with Christopher. He loved it when the Lord laid a message on his heart. He was still the pastor on call at Protestant Hospital in Nashville, and had been since 1942. There was a time Christopher quit preaching when his first wife died, but the calling recommenced in him shortly after he met Jerilyn in December, 1941.

As they walked from their home to Christmas Hotel, they greeted friends also walking to one of the churches on the square or to Christmas Hotel. Most of the residents who lived close to the square walked, if they were of able body. Even with the snow on the ground, it was much more convenient than driving and trying to find a parking spot. Not only did many of the guests at Christmas Hotel attend Sunday service at Christmas, but many of the townspeople attended, also.

As the family entered the hotel, they were greeted by many attendees waiting in the lobby. Sheriff Darius Scott and his wife Barbara were there, too. There was so much snow on the ground that the Scotts decided it was best not to drive to Bowling Green to the Methodist church where they were members – where Lucy had attended with her mama.

The Wrights greeted the morning desk clerk, Patrick Mullins, and those waiting in the lobby. The giant Christmas tree in the lobby already had many gifts around it. Some of the gifts were from the hotel staff to the Wrights, but the majority of the gifts were from the Wrights to the hotel staff. Hanging along the mantle of the huge fireplace, they read the names on their stockings: Christopher, Jerilyn, Lily, Ken, and Carrie Emeline. By Christmas Eve, those stockings would be bulging with small gifts.

As soon as the family arrived, Lily immediately sat down at the organ to play the selected hymns as the congregation gathered. Even Lucy sang out with a beautiful soprano voice that surprised the family. They had not heard her sing. Even when they sang along to the records while in the McLemore's wagon and decorating the tree, she did not sing loudly. They wondered at the times if she knew the words. However, this morning Lucy appeared happy and enjoyed the music.

*****

Jerilyn could see that every day Lucy's heart healed a little more, but she knew that might not last. Tonight they must tell her that the court had ordered her to be turned over to her next of kin. No matter how hard this was on them, it was going to be much harder on Lucy. They feared Lucy was entering "the lion's den," but this morning they hoped she would have a happy memory of being in church with the Wright family and their friends and hotel guests.

Pastor Christopher Wright stood at the pulpit. "We are still six days from Christmas, so I will not read the Christmas Story until Christmas Eve on Friday evening. I invite all of you to return at six o'clock in the evening of Christmas Eve for the traditional candlelight service. Our family will be caroling around Franklin after that service, and anyone is welcome to join us." He asked the congregation in the chapel and those overflowing into the lobby to find Matthew chapter 11 and verses 28-30 in their Bibles. "Please stand for the reading of God's Word.

"*Come unto me, all ye that labour and are heavy laden, and I will give you rest. Take my yoke upon you, and learn of me; for I am meek and lowly in heart: and ye shall find rest unto your souls. For my yoke is easy, and my burden is light.*'"

Lucy looked up at Jerilyn with a huge smile. Jerilyn was not expecting a smile, and felt somewhat confused, but Lucy appeared pleased about the message the Lord was to present through Christopher.

*****

Lucy was remembering a time with her mama at the Methodist Church on State Street in Bowling Green. The verses were familiar to her because that was the day her mama said she found Jesus. Lucy vividly remembered her mama that morning. Her mama began to tremble and then she cried. Lucy watched as her mama removed the handkerchief from her purse and blew her nose. She could not stop crying through the sermon. When the pastor gave the altar call, her mama asked her to wait, and she walked forward. She did not run away this time. Lucy watched as the pastor's wife prayed with her mama. When they finished praying, the pastor's wife spoke to her husband. The pastor joyfully announced to the congregation that Rose Clark had just asked the Lord Jesus to come into her heart and save her. Rose Clark was now a child of God.

Later at home, Lucy asked her mama what that meant, and her mama replied with, "All my burdens have been lifted. The Lord Jesus saved my soul today, forgave me of my sins, and now I will eternally dwell with Him. I want that for you, too, honey. I hope someday you will ask Jesus into your heart, and you will forgive me, too, Lucy. I have fallen short as your mama."

Her mama had cried again when she hugged Lucy. Lucy did not understand what her mama needed to be forgiven for, and did not understand what sins had to be forgiven, and she said so.

"Someday you will," her mama replied.

The church gave her mama a Bible that evening when she was baptized. Her mama talked about it for days and read the verses over and over to Lucy from her Bible until they both had them memorized. Discussing with Lucy what the verses meant to her, she admitted to Lucy she was very tired and that she had been carrying a huge burden. Lucy didn't understand burden, but her mama explained it was something she had done wrong and the sin was eating at her. She explained to Lucy that a yoke was a crossbar that encircled the necks of a pair of oxen, so that the oxen could pull heavy loads.

Her mama felt as though she had a yoke around her neck and that she had pulled a heavy load after her beloved husband Leonard died. However, the Lord said He was going to give her rest. The yoke of the Lord was easy and His burden was light. Her mama said she needed to lighten her load. She needed to give her heart to Him. She needed rest. She needed to be forgiven of her sins. She also needed to rectify a major sin. Lucy wasn't sure what that meant either.

The following week, her mama eagerly repeated the message to everyone who would listen. She talked to the patrons and the staff at the State Theater. She talked to Uncle Otto and Aunt Eula Mae, but they didn't want to hear about it. Aunt Eula Mae had a few things to say to her sister. 'You 'member what it was like when we was growin' up? We barely had clothes an food. War was God then? Our mama dint even knowed who ar daddy was. War was God then? How bout Mama's boyfriends that tried to bother us when Mama was passed out drunk? War was God then? We had ta do ar own fightin'. Thar was no God ta help us. Otto had it no better. His drunken mama an papa beat on him an his brothers an sisters evry minute. They never could do nuthin right. They was kicked aroun worse than dogs! War was God then? So, sister, ya can tek

His heavy loads an burdens an shove 'em. I doan wunt nothing ta do wif Him!'

Lucy remembered that her mama cried that night because she had hoped to get through to her sister, but her sister had what her mama called a hard heart, and only God could soften it. She heard her mama pray that night to ask God to someday soften her sister's heart. She wanted her sister in eternity with her. She prayed for Uncle Otto, for Lucy and her four cousins. She said she was sorry, even though she was not a Christian at the time, that she had not even discussed God with her beloved husband Leonard. She said she didn't know if Leonard was saved or not. All she knew was that he didn't go to church.

However, Lucy's mama thanked God she had met Leonard. Leonard did come from a decent and well educated family, and he drew her away from the devastating life she was living. She thanked God she was able to leave her mama and sister and move to Nashville. If she had stayed with them, she probably would never have gone to college and nurse's training. She would never have bettered herself. She would never have met Leonard.

However, she still had a dilemma and only the Lord could help her. She needed to right a wrong. Lucy remembered her mama asking God to help her.

*****

Following dinner that evening, Christopher and Jerilyn called all four children into the front room. This was difficult for Christopher, but Jerilyn sat beside him, encouraging him while holding his hand. Christopher looked around at all the beautiful and happy faces. Bullet and Daisy lay on the warm hearth in front of the fire. He looked at the Christmas tree and thought about all the happy times in this room. It was in this room that he first began to know Jerilyn. That evening back in December of 1941, he and Jerilyn sat and told stories about their lives before they had met.

When they first met Jerilyn was only twenty, and he was twenty-eight years old. Jerilyn told him about her husband Kenneth Seifert. It was in this room that she also informed him she was carrying her husband Kenneth's child. He told Jerilyn about his wife Ellie who had died giving birth to Lily on Easter Sunday, 1936. Daisy the dog was here then; however, she was only three, and now her bones and joints were old and sore at fifteen. He remembered the birth of the twins in 1942, how he paced this room, worried that Jerilyn might die in childbirth like Ellie. How he prayed that night for Jerilyn and her baby. Not only did Jerilyn live, but God gave them two babies.

Then Christopher also remembered the sad

times, when his and Jerilyn's only child together was kidnapped on Christmas morning, 1946 from the nursery at Protestant Hospital in Nashville. They sat together in this room, on this very sofa, looking at the same Christmas tree decorations, with Daisy on the hearth, praying and crying out to God for their missing child. The hospital and the Nashville police department spent weeks trying to figure out what happened to newborn Lydia Grace, but the leads came up cold. Then he remembered the nights they cried over Jerilyn's two miscarriages in the years following the kidnapping. This room held happy times and sad times. Tonight would be another sad time.

"We have brought all of you here tonight to discuss a matter regarding Lucy's future," Christopher began. "As you know, your mom and I have tried to get Lucy admitted into an orphanage, one local and one in Louisville, in hopes that she could be adopted by a proper family. However, we recently learned her Uncle Otto and Aunt Eula Mae want her to come and live with them."

He and Jerilyn watched as Lucy's face changed from smiles to horror and then sadness. He hurt for the little girl but knew he must say something uplifting. "Lucy, they are your family and if they now want you to live with them, I pray it's because they love you. They are the closest relatives to your mama, so the judge feels he should award you to them. We, as a family, would like to celebrate this last evening with you."

Christopher held Jerilyn's hand as they observed the downcast faces of their own children. Their children clearly did not want Lucy to return to her aunt and uncle. Lucy had already told them stories about them and her cousins, and Christopher was sure the stories were not pleasant. "Sheriff Scott will be returning you to your aunt and uncle in the morning, but tonight we can sing Christmas carols together."

"Will I be able ... to take Bullet ... with me?" asked Lucy, as she struggled with the question. Her little face held the saddest expression and she looked as though she would cry at any moment.

"At this time, I think Bullet will be able to go with you. Sheriff Scott plans to pick you up, along with Bullet in the morning."

"May I come and visit all of you sometime?"

This time Jerilyn answered. "I hope that can be arranged with your aunt and uncle. After you're settled in, we will speak to them about visitations. We also insist you take all your new clothes with you. You will be able to re-enroll after the first of the year in your old class in Bowling Green Elementary. You may even have the same teacher. Won't that be wonderful, Lucy?"

"Sure," was Lucy's first response. "I do like Mrs. Deaton's class, though. She lets me help her. I get to pass out papers and read. I like to read aloud to the class. Mrs. Deaton is really nice."

"I know you like her, honey," said Jerilyn. "If your aunt and uncle don't take you to the library to get books and read, maybe we can make arrangements to do that with you each week."

"Okay," Lucy said, clearly disheartened.

Christopher walked to the piano and sat down. He motioned for Lily to join him on the bench. She had taken lessons from her father since around age three. Christopher played beautifully and had learned from his own mother who taught piano to many children in Franklin and around Simpson County. Now, hoping to cheer up the family, he wanted to change the subject. "Well, if there are no more questions, let's do something fun and sing some Christmas Carols. I know 'O Little Town of Bethlehem' is Lily's favorite, so we can start there, and then others can choose the next Christmas Carol."

Christopher played with Lily beside him also playing and the others joined in, but not with the normal enthusiasm. *This will be a long night*, thought Christopher.

Chapter Sixteen

The Long Drive

"Fear thou not; for I am with thee: be not
dismayed; for I am thy God: I will strengthen
thee; yea, I will help thee; yea, I will uphold thee
with the right hand of my righteousness."
Isaiah 41:10

Monday morning
December 20, 1954
During the drive from Franklin to Bowling Green, Sheriff Scott observed Lucy and Bullet in his rearview mirror while they rode in the back of his cruiser. Lucy stared out the window with the saddest expression he had ever seen on any child's face, and hers was tear-streaked from earlier. The dog was stretched out, taking up most of the back seat. Lucy petted him absentmindedly. The drive seemed to take much longer than it normally did. Lucy's sorrow broke Darius's heart.

Darius Scott had worked in the sheriff's department since he graduated high school. It was the only occupation of which he ever dreamed. He hung around the sheriff's office as a young child. At the time, his uncle was the deputy sheriff, and sometimes he took Darius out in the cruiser. Those were the best memories of his childhood. While his friends were playing baseball or basketball, Darius just wanted to spend his time with the sheriff and deputy sheriff. He even washed their cars in the garage every Saturday.

He liked being a sheriff in a small town. There was much less crime than in the big cities. Before he married Barbara, his high school sweetheart, she asked him if he planned to move to Louisville or Lexington or Nashville. He said his intentions were to serve Franklin if he won the election for deputy sheriff, and then later become sheriff when his uncle retired. He knew Barbara was relieved. Franklin was Darius's home, and Franklin was where he would live and die.

Barbara wanted to have several children, but if they lived in a bigger city, because of the higher crime rate, she feared raising children by herself if something happened to him. She thought his chances were much better in a small town. However, after seventeen years of marriage, their dream to have children had dimmed over the years.

Darius didn't have many disturbing situations to deal with. Every now and then he had to settle a dispute, usually over something inconsequential. There was no alcohol allowed in Simpson County and that helped his job a great deal. However, he knew some of the men drove the six miles over the border into Tennessee and brought it back. Friday nights were not always pleasant. All-in-all, being a sheriff in Simpson County was the job he always wanted.

Today was the hardest assignment he had ever been given. He watched Lucy again in the rearview mirror. This was going to be difficult, but as his friend Judge John James, Jr. said, 'the law's the law.'

Darius pulled up to a parking space in front of *Tandy's Billiards*. Christopher had told him earlier that morning that there was an entrance around back, so he would not have to take Lucy and the dog through the billiard parlor.

He opened the back door of his cruiser, helped Lucy out, and picked up her suitcase. Bullet hopped out and waited dutifully beside Lucy. Darius watched as Lucy looked up at the window above the billiard parlor. The curtain quickly closed. She sighed and looked down at the ground. He had a fleeting thought to put Lucy and Bullet back in the cruiser and take off, but he knew that would just make matters worse.

The three of them walked around back. Darius and Lucy waited as Bullet relieved himself, then they climbed the steps to the rear balcony. Darius held the back door for Lucy and Bullet to enter, and followed them into the dimly lit hallway.

Lucy pointed to the door. "That's where Uncle Otto and Aunt Eula Mae live."

The rickety old door opened before Darius could knock. A man and woman stood in the doorway with four disheveled children in the rear. "Mornin', Shurff!" said the man. "I suppose you brung ar sweet lil Lucy home ta us. Ma lil woman here was missin' her sumpin' awful!" He hugged the woman at his side.

"Ma name's Otto Smith and this here's ma wife Eula Mae. Come in, Shurff, an' meet the young 'uns."

Darius, Lucy and Bullet cautiously stepped into the room. Darius observed the seedy room, aware that Otto was eyeing Bullet cautiously.

"This here's ma sons Junior and Willie, an' ma daughters Sadie and Hazel."

The children looked indifferently at Darius and didn't say a word.

Otto eyed Bullet again. "Lucy, honey, we didn't expect the dog. Ar ya plannin' to keep him here?"

Darius answered for Lucy. "She's been through a great deal of distress with the passing of her mama. The dog offers her comfort. Mr. and Mrs. Christopher Wright beg you to allow Lucy to keep the dog.

"Of course, Shurff. It's not a problem,"

answered Otto, his fake smile revealing tobacco stained teeth.

"I would like to speak to Lucy privately for a moment before I leave her in your custody." Darius stepped back into the hallway with Lucy and Bullet and closed the door. He pulled out a paper and pencil and began to write. When he spoke it was in a whisper, so that her aunt and uncle would not hear. "Lucy, I know the Wrights gave you their home phone number and the phone number at Christmas Hotel to call collect, but I'm going to give you my phone numbers, too." He tore off the paper. "These are my numbers at home and the office. I noticed a phone booth in front of *Tandy's Billiards*. You call me collect if you can't reach the Wrights. I'll be there for you if there is *any* problem at all. If you need me, please call. Also, my wife Barbara works at the Methodist church where you attended with your mama. You can also get help weekdays from her."

Lucy took the paper and slipped it in her pocket with the numbers the Wrights had given her earlier that morning.

Darius knocked on the door to signify the private meeting with Lucy was over.

Otto opened the door. "Come in, darlin'. Yer home now!" He held his arms wide open.

Darius cringed as Lucy and Bullet entered the

apartment.

"Thank ya, Shurff. We won't be needin' ya now," At that statement, he slammed the damaged door.

"God, *please* take care of Lucy," Darius prayed aloud.

Chapter Seventeen

Compromise

*"But if any provide not for his own, and specially
for those of his own house, he hath denied the
faith, and is worse than an infidel."*
1 Timothy 5:8

Tuesday morning
December 21, 1954
Lucy lay curled up on a pillow in the corner of the Smiths' living room with Bullet beside her. Her aunt and uncle had become very cold toward her as soon as Sheriff Scott left. They had given her a thin blanket the night before, and made it plain she was not a welcome member of the family. The two bedrooms and the sofas were for the immediate family. Bullet was her only comfort. He lay beside her through the night. Uncle Otto grudgingly allowed him to sleep in the apartment.

Lucy didn't move even though the morning light streamed through the dirty window. Everyone was still asleep. Her aunt and uncle slept in one of the bedrooms, Sadie and Hazel in another, and Junior and Willie slept on the two sofas in the living room.

Her aunt and uncle had stayed up late in the kitchen talking, drinking the sickening liquor, and chewing and spitting the nasty tobacco. She thought back on their conversation last night, while she had tried to sleep.

"We're goin' ta see them Wrights agin in the mornin'," her uncle had said. "They needs ta give us the money fer the gurl and ta keep thet dog."

"I doan know, Otto. They's awful uppity," said her aunt. "They may be too highin mighty ta give us money."

"They will if we tellim we won't feed her or thet mangy hound. They'll come aroun."

Lucy's suitcase sat beside her, along with her coat. The night before, her aunt and uncle had looked into the suitcase.

"Whewee!" her aunt had said. "Lookit the clothes Miss Priss has. Ain't she gonna be all purty in these here dresses. It's too bad they won't fit Sadie and Hazel. An lookit this new coat. They's even a matchin' hat and a fur muff. Ain't Miss Priss all special! Lookit those shiny patent leather shoes and furry boots. My, my...."

The cousins taunted her, also, until they all fell asleep. She thought they might destroy her new clothes, but fortunately they didn't. She also feared they might be scared of Bullet and send him away. She knew Uncle Otto was mean, but he had cautiously stepped around Bullet throughout the night.

*****

While everyone slept this morning, Lucy knew she needed to let Bullet out to hunt for some breakfast and relieve himself. She realized the aunt and uncle wouldn't feed him, let alone give him some scraps.

She quietly rose from the pillow with Bullet protectively at her side. She was careful not to awaken Junior and Willie, who were still sprawled on the sofas. She slipped on her coat, hat, scarf, boots, and mittens, and carefully opened the old rickety door. Bullet followed her. She quietly closed the door and stepped into the hallway. She looked over to the door that led to where she had lived with her mama.

"Oh, Mama," she said aloud, "I miss you so much."

She looked back at Bullet and continued to the door that led to the balcony. As soon as she opened the door, Bullet ran down the steps and took care of his business. Lucy quickly followed and entered the outdoor privy. When she finished, Bullet was waiting for her, wagging his tail. The apartment had a small bathroom, but she didn't want to use it. The outdoor privy was actually cleaner.

"Bullet, go and hunt for your breakfast," she commanded, pointing to the field, and further away, the woods behind the field. He hesitated and then headed toward the field and woods. Lucy smiled. *At least Bullet will have breakfast.* She turned and climbed the steps. When she reached the top, she looked back over the field. *I hope he'll come back after he's eaten. I certainly wouldn't come back here if I hadn't been ordered to do so.*

Instead of going into her aunt and uncle's apartment, she headed towards her old apartment where she had lived with her mama. She didn't know if it had been rented or not, and she had not been back there since her mama died. She gently knocked, but no one answered. She turned the knob and it was unlocked, so she stepped into the apartment. She left the outside balcony door and the apartment door ajar so Bullet could find her when he returned.

She walked through the apartment remembering her mama. In the bedroom, she looked at the bed where her mama had died. It was now stripped of the linens and blankets. Lucy could not help herself. The tears began to flow. Most of her mama's clothes were gone from the closet. She knew some would fit Aunt Eula Mae, and Lucy remembered her aunt picking over the better clothes the morning her mama died. In the living room sat a scarred table in front of the window. That was where Mama placed the Christmas tree. It would not have had bubble lights and lovely ornaments like the tree she helped decorate at the Wrights' home, but it would still have been pretty. She and her mama always strung popcorn and cranberries and glued paper chains out of red and green construction paper. They wrapped the paper chains like garland around the tree and also around the perimeter of the room where the wall and ceiling met, and around the door frames. They would turn out the lights in the ceilings and lamps, light the candles, and sing Christmas songs. It was special to them. She wiped the tears that ran down her face. Her aunt and uncle had not put up a tree and she saw no Christmas presents, even for her cousins. There would be no Christmas for her this year; no Christmas for Lucy. She sat on the floor and continued to cry softly.

Bullet found her as he nudged the door open enough to accommodate his big body to pass through. He walked up to Lucy and licked the tears from her face. She put her arms around his massive neck. "I love you, Bullet," she said to him, while crying some more into his fur. "Please don't leave me, Bullet."

Her aunt and uncle appeared in the doorway. Bullet growled in a low and ominous way. "Get that flea bitten hound outta here," ordered her uncle, but he backed up and lowered his voice when he said it. "We're goin' out and we doan want him in either 'partment no more. He can stay outside, or in the hall."

They turned and walked out the door to the balcony.

Her cousins stood in the doorway of their apartment. Lucy knew she didn't want to go back in there, so she chose to walk to the square with Bullet. *I can't lose Bullet. He's my only friend.*

*****

Within the hour, Otto and Eula Mae pulled their rusty old jalopy in front of Christmas Hotel, parked, and entered the lobby. They both strutted up to the front desk, feeling very important as they confronted Christopher.

"Is Lucy okay?" Christopher asked with concern.

"Sure. Ar sweet lil niece is jus fine," answered Otto with a smirk on his face. "We's here ta talk about her upkeep ... and thet dog. They's mighty 'spensive ta feed. My lil woman an I thought you an yer wife would like to hep wif the food," he said, as he hugged Eula Mae to his side and chewed his chaw of tobacco.

Jerilyn walked out of the office behind the check-in desk and stood beside Christopher.

Eula Mae presented her best fake smile and added, "Yeah, we thought since y'all was so fond of her, you'd want ta hep out. We'll even let ya visit wif her."

"That sounds like bribery," Christopher said. "I don't think you want to get the sheriff involved, do you?"

Otto didn't miss a beat. "I doan think ya want the gurl ta starve, do ya?" He smiled again with the same smirk along with a wink.

"Let me speak to my wife in private. Stay right here," ordered Christopher in a stern voice.

"Doan try any funny business," Otto fired back, just as stern as Christopher. "Y'all have one minute or we's leavin' and the offer is over."

Christopher turned and led Jerilyn back into the office.

"Christopher, I don't think we have a choice. We're going to need to help them so we can see Lucy. I want to ensure she's eating properly and not being mistreated."

"I want the same thing, Jerilyn, but I won't give those people cash. We'll buy groceries and personally deliver them. I don't want to support their drinking and tobacco habit. We'll tell them that we'll buy the groceries three times a week. In return, they must let us visit privately with Lucy each time we deliver the groceries, *and* we will take her to church each Sunday."

"I agree. We can send them on their way now,

and deliver some groceries early this afternoon."

Christopher and Jerilyn approached Otto and Eula Mae with the offer.

"We'd like money an buy ar own groceries," said Otto in a gruff tone.

Christopher answered in the same tone. "You'll get the groceries we buy and like it. Mrs. Wright and I will deliver them in a few hours, *and* we expect to see Lucy *and* Bullet."

Otto and Eula Mae grudgingly accepted the offer and left in a hurry.

Christopher called his assistant manager to let him know they needed him to watch the Christmas Hotel desk. He and Jerilyn walked home to pick up the station wagon. Within an hour they were shopping at the *Piggly Wiggly*. They loaded the car with ten bags of food. They bought meat, chicken, and fish, along with canned, fresh, and frozen vegetables, canned and frozen fruit, flour, cornmeal, sugar, salt, pepper, four dozen eggs, bacon, sausage, butter, lard, olive oil, vinegar, packaged desserts, several loaves of bread, and several gallons of milk, tea bags, along with a fifty pound bag of dog chow. "This should more than suffice for when we return on Thursday," said Jerilyn.

"I imagine they don't have a regular food supply," responded Christopher. "Their own four children probably have never had a proper meal. I wonder if Eula Mae even knows how to cook ... or cares."

They drove up in front of *Tandy's Billiards* and parked. Christopher turned to Jerilyn, "Let's leave the groceries in the car until we check on Lucy."

As they closed the car doors, they saw the curtain part in the upstairs apartment and quickly close. "Do those people constantly sit and look out that window?" asked Christopher disapprovingly. They walked around back and up the stairs. They entered the hallway and knocked on the door.

One of the boys answered the door. He didn't say anything, but just looked at them.

Christopher spoke first. "May we speak to your father?"

The boy turned and stepped back as his father walked out of what was probably one of the bedrooms. Christopher saw the protrusion in his jaw and realized he had another wad of tobacco in his mouth.

"Whare're the groceries?" the man asked in an angry voice, as he walked across the room scratching his bare and hairy chest. He had obviously been napping.

"Do these people ever work?" Christopher said sarcastically under his breath to Jerilyn.

"The groceries are in my car," answered

Christopher. "We want to see Lucy first."

"She ain't here. We las seen her this mornin'."

This time Jerilyn asked, "You mean you returned here several hours ago and you didn't feel the responsibility to make sure she was all right?"

Christopher knew Jerilyn's mother's heart was furious, but he also knew they must remain calm, or Otto might refuse the visits. He took Jerilyn's hand and tried again to talk to Otto. "Where do you think she might be?"

"This mornin' she was across the hall in her daid mama's apartment wif thet dog. I told her to get the dog out an keep him out!"

Christopher had a retort, but kept it to himself. He bit his lip. "The sooner we find Lucy, the sooner you'll get the groceries. Would you ask your children to help us find her?"

"Sure. You kids go look fer the brat."

Christopher and Jerilyn did their best to remain calm. Due to the circumstances, it would do Lucy no good to blow up at her aunt and uncle.

The four children hurried to don their ill-fitting worn-out coats. They rushed out the door and Otto slammed it behind them. Christopher noticed the door was insecure, with several cracks. It undoubtedly was in need of repair, or merely replaced, because of the abuse it received from this family.

The six of them stepped out on the balcony. "Do you children have any idea where Lucy may be?" asked Christopher.

The children looked at Christopher as though sizing him up. Christopher realized they were probably never called children, and maybe he had misjudged them. After all, they could not help who their parents were. It's not like you can choose your parents, and these children had drawn the short straw. If Otto and Eula Mae treated them as they treated Lucy, they were probably called brats or worse. Only God knew what negative words had been drummed into their fragile young minds.

"First, what are your names?" Jerilyn asked in a kind voice.

They each answered her question.

"I'm Junior and I'm the oldest," the first one answered proudly, poking his chest with his thumb.

"I'm Sadie and I'm next." She raised her hand toward the sky.

"I'm Willy."

"I'm Hazel and I'm the youngest."

Christopher guessed at their ages. They looked to range from about fourteen or fifteen down to nine or ten. They weren't smart-mouthed or rude when they were away from their parents. What a terrible life to live, he thought.

"I saw her go to the fountain this morning," said

Willy politely, and in answer to Christopher's question.

"I saw her at the manger scene at the Methodist Church on State Street," said Sadie.

"She played tug-o-war with an old rope out in the field with Bullet," said Junior.

"She's good friends with Bullet," commented Hazel.

"Okay, we would very much appreciate your help. Junior, would you and Hazel walk around the fountain and look for her?" asked Christopher.

They nodded yes and each said, "Yes, sir."

"Willie and Sadie, would you both please check the field?" asked Christopher.

"Yes, sir," they answered courteously.

Christopher was amazed at the turnaround in their behavior. "Mrs. Wright and I will go to the Methodist Church on State Street. Watch the clock in the courthouse tower, and we'll meet back here in approximately thirty minutes. Okay?"

"Yes, sir," said Junior. He turned to his three siblings. "Come on, let's go!"

Christopher and Jerilyn watched the children scatter, then he and Jerilyn walked to the church.

In front of the Methodist church stood the manger scene Lucy described. They saw the sign around the side for the church office, so that was where they began their search. A woman sat typing at the desk with her back to them. When she turned, they saw it was Barbara, Darius's wife. "Hi, Barbara, we didn't know you were working here," Jerilyn said.

Barbara stood and hugged them both. "Actually, I just began work here as the church secretary about five months ago. What brings you two to Bowling Green?"

They told her briefly about Lucy and why they were there. She nodded. "Darius told me about having to deliver her to the aunt and uncle yesterday. He said it was the worst day he ever experienced as sheriff. My heart goes out to that poor little girl, losing her mama and all. I met Rose Clark briefly here at church. I typed her Certificate of Baptism back in August. We were all saddened to hear about her untimely death. That little girl deserves better."

"We agree," said Christopher. "Right now, we need to find her and make sure she's all right. We have groceries for the family, but we're not giving her aunt and uncle the groceries until we see her."

"Well, I might be able to help in that regard. She was here this morning with a huge dog. I told her that our church had taken up a donation and there was now a monument at the Fairview Cemetery for her mama where Rose was buried. The monument is in the first section and near the front gate. As you're probably aware, the first section is nearly full, and so the city has recently purchased land across Fairview Avenue for future graves. The new cemetery may not open until spring, but there was a nice spot left in the first section to bury Rose."

"Thank you, Barbara," said Christopher. "We'll check the cemetery next."

When they stepped outside, Jerilyn asked, "Shouldn't we check in with the children first?"

Christopher looked at his watch. "You're right. We've already been gone close to thirty minutes. Let's meet the children and then drive to Fairview Cemetery. If I remember correctly, the cemetery is only a little over a mile from here."

They met up with the children, who had nothing to report. Christopher told them where they were heading, thanked them for their help, and returned to the car. When they arrived at the cemetery, the sign said it was open until dark. They parked the car by the front gate and looked to the right of the entrance. They quickly spotted Lucy sitting on a bench near the monument, petting Bullet. Bullet heard them approach, ran to them, rearing up on his hind legs and licking each of them in the face. Lucy stood and ran to them, hugging them around the legs.

"Am I going home with you?" she asked eagerly.

Christopher hated to dash her hopes, but of

course he knew they couldn't lie to her either. Instead, they changed the subject and asked about her mama's monument.

"Look," said Lucy pointing to the monument, "isn't it nice? The Methodist church took up a collection and bought it."

They walked toward the monument, and when they were in front of it, Christopher read aloud.

> *"Rose Clark*
> *September 21, 1924 – December 1, 1954*
> *Beloved wife of Leonard Clark.*
> *Beloved Mama of Lucille Grace Clark."*

There was a rose engraved above her name.

"It's beautiful, Lucy," Christopher said softly.

"How long have you been out here?" asked Jerilyn.

Lucy looked down. She answered in a barely audible voice. "Uncle Otto said he didn't want me in the apartment while he was gone. He said he doesn't want Bullet inside the apartment at all, ever. Bullet has to stay outside or in the hallway. I don't know if Uncle Otto's back yet. While they were gone, I played with Bullet in the field and walked to the fountain. Then I wanted to see the Baby Jesus and pray. Do you think the Baby Jesus hears me when I pray?"

Jerilyn bent down and hugged Lucy. "Yes, dear, He hears you. Don't stop praying. He doesn't want you to stop." On a different note, Jerilyn said to her, "By the way, we met your cousins a while ago."

"They don't like me."

"For some reason, I believe your cousins will treat you differently," said Jerilyn. "You just keep praying and you'll see."

Christopher joined in. "We have permission from your uncle to visit you three times a week, and pick you up for church on Sunday. We also brought food for all seven of you, and will do so three times a week. How does that sound?"

"Wonderful!"

"In the meantime, you have Bullet for a friend, and I'm sure he'll look out for you. Are you hungry?"

"Yes, sir. I haven't had anything to eat since you made my breakfast yesterday."

Christopher sighed, looked at Jerilyn and saw the knitted brow and the biting of her lip. He didn't have to ask what she was thinking. "There's a diner on the square. How about we all go in and have a bite to eat. I'm sure Bullet will wait outside for you."

"Thank you, Mr. Christopher."

When they finished their sandwiches, they headed back to the apartment. Jerilyn and

Christopher each carried up a sack of groceries, and Lucy knocked on the door. Sadie answered the door and smiled. She invited them in and asked her brothers and sister to help with the groceries.

Christopher watched the expression on Lucy's face shift from nervousness to amazement. He knew she had never known the cousins to be so kind. They all put on their jackets and retrieved the remaining eight sacks of groceries.

When they entered the apartment and set the groceries on the table, Christopher asked where their parents were. Junior hung his head and said they were down at the local honky-tonk. "They probably won't be home until very late tonight."

Christopher could see that Jerilyn was clearly upset that once again they left not knowing if Lucy was okay. With her eyes she expressed her displeasure to him. They had been together thirteen years, and Christopher had no trouble reading his wife's feelings. He placed his arm around her and hugged her to his side.

He watched as Jerilyn shrugged off her feelings of annoyance, and addressed the matter at hand. "Are you children hungry?" she asked.

"Yes, but we never learned to cook," answered Sadie.

"Well, how would you like your first cooking lesson?"

Sadie smiled, "I would, and Hazel can help! Lucy would probably like to learn, too."

Lucy smiled and nodded.

"All right," said Jerilyn. "Let's do it. You boys can help, too. Mr. Wright cooks, because it's not just a *woman thing*." She laughed. "First, let's clean up the kitchen, so we have plenty of preparation space. I'll run the dish water if Sadie, Hazel, and Lucy can wash the dishes and put them away. You three men can scrub down the stove, cabinets, countertops, and I'll put away all the groceries."

Junior and Willie beamed their pleasure when she referred to them as men.

When everything was clean and organized, Jerilyn set out the makings for a salad, a meat loaf, canned green beans, mashed potatoes, corn bread, and chocolate pudding. She organized the children in groups. She taught the boys how to chop the fresh vegetables for the salad, peel the potatoes, and peel the onions. In a large bowl, Christopher squeezed together the hamburger, canned tomatoes, onions, bread, and some salt and pepper for the meatloaf. He didn't have everything he normally used, but they could make do.

The Smiths did not have a great deal of pots and pans or dishes, but Christopher and Jerilyn were good at improvising. Jerilyn gave Sadie the tea bags and instructed her to start the boiling of the water for tea. As soon as the water boiled, Sadie added the tea bags and allowed the tea to steep. Afterwards, Sadie added plenty of sugar, and let it cool before she poured it in the pitcher. Later, Jerilyn set the pitcher in the Frigidaire to completely chill the sweet tea.

When the oven was hot, Christopher set the meat loaf in the center of the oven. Jerilyn taught the three girls how to make the chocolate pudding while Christopher helped the boys toss the salad. The olive oil and vinegar they purchased at the *Piggly Wiggly* would be the dressing. Sadie boiled the water for the mashed potatoes and Jerilyn showed her how to check the potatoes with a fork to see if they were done. They had no strainer basket, so Jerilyn picked up two pot holders and drained the water off the potatoes through the lid into the sink. Hazel opened three cans of green beans to heat on the stove top.

When the meat loaf was ready to come out of the oven, Jerilyn cranked up the heat to 450 degrees for the cornbread. The Smiths didn't possess a measuring cup, but they did have coffee cups. Jerilyn used the coffee cups to measure the corn meal, oil, and milk. She normally added buttermilk, but she and Christopher hadn't bought it, so she showed the girls how to make their own by adding a tablespoon of vinegar to the milk and let it set a few minutes. It was an adequate substitute.

Jerilyn found a large iron skillet, smeared some lard in it and heated it in the oven. In the meantime, Jerilyn had Lucy add a beaten egg to the batter and mix all together for the cornbread. When the skillet was hot, she picked up the pot holders, set the skillet on the stove, poured the batter in, and the skillet sizzled. She set the skillet back in the oven.

"It should be ready in about twelve or thirteen minutes," she told the children. "We'll just watch as the bread turns golden brown."

Sadie found the potato masher and mashed the potatoes with butter, salt and pepper, and some of the leftover buttermilk. To make gravy, there was no bacon or sausage drippings, but Jerilyn improvised again by using the meatloaf drippings. She showed them how to put the drippings in the skillet, add some flour and stir until smooth. They gradually stirred in the milk and added salt and pepper until it was creamy smooth. The whole dinner was ready, and Jerilyn set the skillet of cornbread on the range top along with the meatloaf, mashed potatoes, gravy, and green beans.

The girls removed the bowl of salad from the Frigidaire, iced the glasses for tea, and set them on the table along with the dinnerware. Jerilyn had them form a line with their plates, and dip up the meal from the stove, cafeteria style. There were not seven chairs around the table, so Willie and Junior went across the hall to get three extra chairs from their Aunt Rose's old apartment.

When they sat down, the Smith children were ready to dive in, but Christopher stopped them. "We must thank the Lord first," he said.

The seven of them held hands around the table. "Dear Heavenly Father, we thank Thee for this wonderful feast and the seven pairs of hands that prepared the food. I thank Thee for allowing Jerilyn and me to meet these five young people. They are Thy children and they all are special. Please let them know how exceptional they are. Guide them and protect them as they move forward toward their futures. In Jesus' name we pray ... amen."

Jerilyn and Lucy added their amens. The other four just raised their heads and looked from Christopher to Jerilyn. Christopher and Jerilyn saw their expressions. These children had probably never been prayed for in their young lives.

That's so sad, thought Christopher. They aren't bad children. They just have never been taught any different.

It was six o'clock when they finished the meal. They put the leftovers in the Frigidaire and cleaned up the kitchen. Before Christopher and Jerilyn left, they gave their phone numbers at home and at the Christmas Hotel to Junior, since he was the oldest. He was instructed to call collect for any emergency, or just for cooking tips. That way, Junior and Lucy both had the phone numbers. Christopher and Jerilyn promised they would arrive with recipes each time they came with groceries. They hugged all five children goodbye, walked into the hallway and petted Bullet.

They watched as Lucy set some dog food and table scraps out in a bowl for Bullet, and then they headed for home to their three children. It was a good day and they were pleased they could do something for these neglected children.

Chapter Eighteen

Judge John James, Jr.

"But whoso shall offend one of these little ones
which believe in me, it were better for him that a
millstone were hanged about his neck, and that he
were drowned in the depth of the sea."
Matthew 18:6

Wednesday afternoon
December 22, 2012
All through the night the snow fell, and there was more than eight inches on the ground by morning. The mail arrived and Christopher and Jerilyn finally received the letter from the Masonic Widow and Orphan Home in Louisville. They were told that because some of their children had been adopted since Thanksgiving, they currently had room for up to six more children. They would need to notify the Masonic Home before Christmas if they planned to send Lucy there, as space filled quickly. Christopher and Jerilyn knew they needed to go back and meet with Judge James again. They decided that was on their agenda this afternoon. They called his secretary and were informed the

judge would meet them in his chambers at four o'clock.

Christopher and Jerilyn donned their heavy coats and pulled on their boots and trudged through the snow, arriving at the courthouse promptly at four. They were escorted to the judge's chambers behind his courtroom. Judge James was dressed informally, having removed his robe which hung on the cherry coat and hat rack. He stood, shook their hands, and motioned for Christopher and Jerilyn to take a seat on a leather sofa, across from two matching high-back leather chairs in front of the fireplace.

Judge James had a very masculine, but cozy office. Directly across from the fireplace a large picture window looked out upon the trees in the square. In front of the picture window stood his large cherry desk with a matching high back leather chair behind it, and two smaller matching leather chairs for clients in front of the desk. On the walls Christopher observed his framed law degree, and a framed copy of the Ten Commandments. Behind the desk, on the cherry credenza, he had proudly sat several pictures of his wife Nell and their beautiful children.

The judge opened the conversation, and Christopher assumed this would be an informal meeting. Christopher was immediately at ease, and saw Jerilyn was, also. After the preliminaries, Judge James got to the point. "I know you two didn't come to chat, so how may I help you?"

Like Sheriff Scott, Judge James was also a school friend of Christopher's, but Christopher knew that he had to uphold the law, irrespective of personal relationships. Lucy's aunt and uncle were the young girl's next of kin.

"Well, John, I need to address the situation again concerning Lucy Clark and also the four children of Mr. and Mrs. Otto Smith. Let me update you as to what has happened since we last spoke. Yesterday, the aunt and uncle came to Christmas Hotel and asked us for money for the upkeep of Lucy and Bullet, or they threatened we wouldn't see them again. We strongly expressed to them that we wouldn't support them with money, but we would bring groceries three times per week. In return, we wanted to visit with Lucy each time, and have permission to take her to church on Sunday. At first Mr. and Mrs. Smith said no, because they wanted the money instead of the food. We let them know in no uncertain terms that groceries would be the only offer. They finally agreed to our terms.

"When we delivered the groceries yesterday, they didn't know where to find Lucy. They didn't have the decency to check on her after over six hours! His four children, Jerilyn, and I scouted the area to find her. The children had three suggestions where she had been earlier that morning. One of the places was the Methodist Church on State Street. By the way, I don't know if you knew, but Darius's wife Barbara is the secretary at the Methodist church."

The judge nodded. "I had heard that from Darius."

"Well," Christopher continued, "Barbara told us the church had donated the monument for Lucy's mama's grave, and she had conveyed that information to Lucy earlier that morning. Barbara suspected that's where we might find Lucy.

"We drove to the cemetery and did indeed find her. We also discovered she had not eaten since the previous morning at seven o'clock when we fed her breakfast. Who knows when she would have been given something to eat, because when we returned to the apartment to deliver the groceries, the Smith children told us their parents had already left for the evening to go to the local honky-tonk on the edge of town. Their own children hadn't eaten either. There was no food in the apartment. I have no idea how those four children have survived. They didn't know how to prepare the food we brought, so Jerilyn and I helped them cook a meal and ate supper with them.

"My point, John, is this is child abuse. Those

two aren't fit to care for Lucy, let alone their own children. They're also a poor influence on the five children. They are morally depraved and the children would be better off without them. When their four children are around them, they are rude and obnoxious like their parents. When the children are not under their parents' influence, they are polite, respectful, and cooperative. In my opinion, I think all five children need to be removed from the home.

"Today, I received a letter from the Masonic Widow and Orphan Home in Louisville. It was in response to the letter I sent them regarding availability for Lucy. They do have room for up to six children at this time, so they would have room for Lucy and the four cousins. However, we would need to request the space for the children before Christmas. We need to move on this situation as soon as possible. Will you help us, John?"

While the judge listened, he stroked his chin, and sat deep in thought, staring into the fire. Finally he turned to face Christopher and Jerilyn, and with a huge sigh he said, "I understand you two have become attached to Lucy, and now probably to her four cousins. I realize the aunt and uncle are probably despicable individuals. As a judge, I can't make hasty decisions. Before I would make a decision to remove children from a home, I would need an extreme offense."

Christopher interrupted. "Don't you think that not providing a child food for thirty hours, and not knowing or caring, I might add, where she was for over six hours, is an extreme offense? What do *you* consider an extreme offense?"

Christopher was becoming angry and Jerilyn placed her hand on his arm, and said softly, "Christopher ... please don't. This won't help Lucy or her cousins."

Judge James took a deep breath. "It's okay, Jerilyn, I understand completely how Christopher ... *and you* must feel. There are agencies that look into this sort of situation when the welfare of a child is concerned. I'll contact one of the judges in Warren County, and have someone sent tomorrow to check the apartment and make an assessment."

*****

While Judge James was signing the order in Simpson County to have the Smiths assessed in Warren County, the four Smith children and Lucy were in their kitchen planning supper. Their parents were getting dressed to go to the honky-tonk again. Sadie pulled a package of seven pork chops from the Frigidaire and set them on the counter. They hoped their mama would like to cook dinner with them before she and their dad left for the evening. After all, they needed to eat, too. Sadie asked the others, "What else would you like with the pork chops?"

Willy immediately said, "Mash potatoes and gravy."

"That's good," said Sadie. "We know how to fix that."

Hazel suggested, "How about some canned peas? And we can cook some fresh carrots to mix with the peas."

"That sounds good, too. I think we can handle that. We can make another salad and we have some left-over cornbread. The only thing I'm not sure of is how to cook the pork chops. Maybe Mama will help us with that."

"What're you kids doin' in the kitchen? You don't know whut yer doin'! Git outa there!" yelled Eula Mae.

"Yes, we do," answered Sadie in a polite tone. "The Wrights helped us make dinner yesterday after you and Daddy left. If you can tell me how to cook the pork chops, I can prepare dinner for all of us." She smiled brightly at her mama hoping that she, her siblings, and Lucy would be appreciated by her parents for their efforts.

"Waddya ya mean the Wrights helped ya?" yelled Otto, stomping into the kitchen.

This time Lucy spoke up. "They own Christmas Hotel and they know all about cooking! They said they'd bring us recipes every time they come and make sure we're eating properly. They're nice people and they want to help all of us," she answered in her innocent way.

"So yer the cause of this, lil Missy," said Eula Mae. "We doan need thar help or you tellin' them what we should and shouldn't do." Eula Mae grabbed Lucy's shoulders and sat her down hard on the kitchen chair.

Lucy's lip trembled as she looked up at her aunt, and said in a very small and frightened voice, "The Wrights were only trying to help."

"Shut yer trap, gurl," said her uncle angrily. "And as fer you four," he said to his own children, "quit gawkin'. I'm sellin some a thet food tonight. Yer mama an I has ar needs, too. We doan need all thet food. Bag mos of it up an we're takin it wif us now." His voice slurred, so they all knew he had already had a few drinks.

"But Daddy—" began Junior.

"Ya shuddup! Ya need ta be taught a lesson!" Otto back-handed Junior, slamming him into the counter. He hit his head on a cabinet and his lower back on the sharp edge of the countertop. Junior slid to the floor. Willy ran to his brother, knelt down beside him; but his brother was knocked unconscious, and the back of his head was bleeding.

"Dad, Junior's hurt!" Willy cried out in alarm.

"Shuddup or I'll teach you a lesson, too," yelled Otto, and his face reddened in rage.

Lucy began to cry and Eula Mae back-handed her across the mouth so hard that her ring cut into Lucy's lip. Her lip spurted blood, and she fell from the chair to the floor. Lucy put her hand to her mouth and cried harder. As she sat slumped on the floor, she looked up at her aunt in fear.

Eula Mae laughed, grabbing Lucy viciously by her hair and yanking her to her feet, only to slap her so hard that she left a bright red hand-print on Lucy's face. Lucy collapsed heavily on to the floor, and curled into the fetal position as she tried to protect herself. Eula Mae's face contorted in a wild rage. Again, she bent down, snatched Lucy's hair and dragged her across the floor while Lucy screamed in pain.

"Stop, Mama!" yelled Sadie. "She's just a little girl and you're hurting her."

Hazel now began to scream, too. "Mama, please stop! You're going to kill her!" she yelled, and burst into tears.

Willy left Junior's side and tried to force his mama away from Lucy, but his mama hit him too, knocking him to the floor. With her other hand she continued to hold Lucy by her hair that was now streaked with blood.

"You ungrateful brat," Eula Mae spat out at

Willy.

They all turned when they heard a loud crash. Bullet burst through the rickety old door and it splintered into hundreds of pieces. He leaped at Eula Mae, viciously biting her arm. She screamed in pain and let loose of Lucy's hair. Bullet growled ferociously, pulling and twisting Eula Mae's arm, while Sadie and Hazel huddled by Junior in shock. Lucy and Willy sat transfixed on the floor where Eula Mae had attacked them.

Otto moved to pull Bullet off his wife, and Bullet turned on him, knocking him to the floor. He bit deeply into Otto's left arm and shook it like a toy. Otto took his right fist and punched it into Bullet's face, but the dog held on, savagely growling and biting and tearing the flesh on Otto's arm. Then Bullet lunged for Otto's throat and Otto put his hands up to protect his face and neck. Bullet bit into Otto's hands, tearing the flesh.

Otto did his best to roll on his stomach, but all he could manage was his side. He was too drunk to fight the dog. The children watched in horror. Bullet repeatedly bit Otto all over his body. The dog was relentless as Otto desperately tried to protect himself, hitting Bullet in vain. It appeared Bullet's rage would not end, and Otto's strength was rapidly dwindling.

Eula Mae ran to the bedroom and grabbed

Otto's revolver. She picked up an empty whiskey bottle in her other hand, and she ran back into the living room. She knocked the bottle over Bullet's head, temporarily stunning the dog. In the meantime, she placed the revolver in Otto's right hand. Otto raised the revolver and fired.

*****

Later that evening, and just before bedtime, the Wrights looked out the window as the snow continued to fall. The radio report said they were under blizzard conditions. The winds had been measured at seventy-five miles per hour and the temperature had dropped to twenty-eight degrees. The predictions were to expect huge snow drifts in the morning and temperatures in the low twenties.

Jerilyn put her arm around Christopher's waist. "Tomorrow we're supposed to take the groceries to the Smiths. I'm worried the car won't get through the snow."

"I think we'll be okay with the chains on the tires. Usually blizzards don't last more than ten hours and this one has gone on for the past five. However, I'm worried that the Smiths have left the children again. The children haven't called, and that concerns me. I thought they might call tonight." He walked to the phone and picked up the receiver. He dialed the operator, but said nothing. He placed the receiver back in the cradle. "Well, even if they need us, they can't get through. The line is dead."

"Christopher, Judge James signed the papers for the Smiths to be assessed. The weather might be too bad tomorrow for that to happen."

"Don't worry, honey, we'll just have to cross that bridge when we come to it. Hopefully, we'll discover that instead of going to the honky-tonk, Otto and Eula Mae have cooked and eaten dinner with the children tonight. We can only pray that all will turn out well." He pulled Jerilyn close to him.

Chapter Nineteen

The Long Night

"And the LORD shall help them, and deliver them: he shall deliver them from the wicked, and save them, because they trust in him."
Psalm 37:40

Thursday morning, one o'clock
December 23, 1954
Lucy lay huddled against Bullet in the igloo her cousins had made. She couldn't sleep, and thought back to the events after Uncle Otto shot Bullet.

*****

Bullet yelped in pain, falling to the floor, and struggled to stand. Blood gushed from his body.

Otto laid the revolver on the floor and Willy quickly grabbed it. He and Sadie ran outside to hide it. Lucy watched in a daze. It just didn't seem real. Her beloved Bullet was in pain because he was trying to protect her. She managed to stand, and on wobbly legs she walked to Bullet. She couldn't tell where he was shot. There was blood everywhere. She was in a daze when she heard Junior groan. He woke up and held the back of his head; blood running down on the collar of his shirt. He stood on

155

unsteady legs and allowed Hazel to wash his head at the sink with a kitchen towel.

Eula Mae screamed at Lucy. "See what you've caused, lil Missy! None of this woudna happened if hadn't been fer you and thet dog. You an thet dog – bof a ya – git outta here!" she shrieked in rage, as blood trailed down her arm. Eula Mae knelt down beside Otto who writhed in pain on the floor.

By then Willy and Sadie had returned and heard what their mama said to Lucy. They hurriedly put on Lucy's coat, hat, mittens and scarf, and their own. Sadie grabbed a clean towel for Lucy's lip, and three blankets. Lucy and Sadie watched as Bullet fought to stand, and they, along with Willy, helped Bullet down the back steps. Willy walked backwards down the steps in front of Bullet and half held the big dog so he wouldn't fall down the steps, while Lucy and Sadie walked on either side of Bullet. They made it to the bottom of the steps and Bullet fell again.

"He's losing a lot of blood," Sadie observed. "We need to stop the blood and get him warm."

The door at the top of the steps slammed, and Junior and Hazel hurried down the steps. Junior had a pair of pants thrown over his shoulder, and a towel wrapped around his head. When they reached the others, Sadie asked Junior if his head had quit bleeding.

"Just about. I'm more concerned about Bullet and Lucy."

"I brought wet and dry towels for Lucy and Bullet," said Hazel.

"Let's get Bullet under the street light and wipe him down," said Sadie. "We need to see about stopping the blood."

The wind was raging and the snow made it difficult to see a foot in front of them. The five of them managed to get Bullet moving, and they finally made it to the streetlight. Sadie told Junior she and Willy had hidden the revolver under the privy. "With this snow, it'll probably be spring before it's ever found," said Sadie.

"Good! I'm glad it's out of the apartment," said Junior. "He can't shoot anyone else like he just did Bullet. I don't trust either one of them after what they did to Lucy, Willy, and me."

They checked Lucy's lip first, and pressed the towel to it so the bleeding would subside, knowing it would be swollen, along with her face. They then washed Bullet as best as they could, but the blood kept flowing. The wound appeared to be in his shoulder and close to his neck. They wrapped him in some of the dry towels and applied pressure.

"We need to get him warm, but I don't know how," said Sadie.

"I do!" Lucy said excitedly. "The Wright family

taught me how to build an igloo and it was warm inside – well, warmer than standing out here in the wind." She explained to them how it was done.

"Lucy, here's the plan," said Junior. "First, put on these old pants of Willy's. They may be big, but they will help keep you warm."

Lucy did as she was told.

"Sadie, Willy and I will go out in the field and build the igloo, while you and Hazel keep applying pressure on Bullet's wound and your lip. The three of you huddle together by the wall. We'll be back to get you as soon as we're finished."

Lucy watched as they grabbed three of the six snow shovels propped against the outside wall. The shovels evidently belonged to *Tandy's Billiards*.

In less than thirty minutes they returned.

"Lucy, it's big enough for you and Bullet to spend the night. You're right. I went inside and it's warm ... at least warmer than out here, and you'll be out of the wind. How's Bullet?"

Lucy removed the towel and the wound still bled, but not gushing as before, and Bullet's breath now sounded labored as he lay in the snow.

"Well, we don't have far to walk. Let's get him on his feet," said Junior.

The boys half carried Bullet, and he hobbled on three legs. Bullet would not go in the igloo until Lucy did. Even in his pain, she realized, he's going to do his best to protect me. The cousins handed Lucy the remaining clean towels and promised to return as soon as they were able, with some food, water and more towels. They laid one blanket on the floor of the igloo so Lucy and Bullet didn't have to lie directly on the snow.

"Keep the pressure on his wound, Lucy, and keep the extra blankets around both of you," said Sadie. She removed her sweater from under her coat and told Hazel to do the same. "Put these sweaters on under your coat so you'll have some more layers," Sadie added.

"I will. Thank you all for your help. I love you all."

Sadie began to cry. "I love you, too, Lucy. I'm sorry we were so mean to you," she choked.

The others expressed similar statements.

"I forgive you," said Lucy. She watched the cousins leave and turned to Bullet. As she applied the pressure to the wound, she talked to him. "I love you, Bullet. Thank you for saving me. I'm sorry you got hurt."

He raised his massive head, licked her cheek, and laid his head back down. She curled up to him, and they tried to keep each other warm in their igloo.

*****

Lucy didn't sleep, but kept applying the pressure. Her body was tired, but for the past few hours she used her body for the pressure on Bullet's wound, lying against him with only a towel between them. She heard voices coming and saw a light beam. The snow continued to fall and the wind howled.

"Lucy, it's us," called Sadie, loudly enough to be heard above the wind.

"We brought you some hot chocolate, vegetable soup, and bread. We brought Bullet some water, and some of his food softened with water," said Junior.

"How's Bullet?" asked Willy.

Lucy sat up. She still had not fallen asleep. She listened to Bullet's labored breathing. "I'm not sure. He's breathing hard and I can't see if the bleeding stopped or not. His body jerks every now and then. What time is it?" she asked, as she took a sip of the hot chocolate.

"It's one o'clock," said Junior. "Move the towel and I'll shine the light on his wound."

Lucy removed the towel and set the water and food by Bullet's head. He lifted his head, sniffed them, but didn't drink or eat. His head dropped back to the ground.

Junior and Sadie examined the wound and then looked at each other. The blood was still bright red and flowing freely. "Put the towel back on the wound, Lucy," said Sadie.

"What happened when you went back to the apartment?" asked Lucy.

Sadie answered in the dim light. Lucy could barely see her face. "First we went to the phone booth in front of *Tandy's Billiards* to try and call Mr. and Mrs. Wright, but their phone was dead. Then we tried Sheriff Scott, but his line was dead, too. The telephone lines must be down from the blizzard."

Junior continued for Sadie. "Then we all went back to the apartment. Daddy and Mama were still fire mad, but they just told us to pack up the food, because they were still going out to sell it. Daddy and Mama had washed their dog bites, and wrapped them. They told us to hang a blanket or sheet in the doorway and make sure nobody from the pool hall wandered in while they were gone, because they didn't want anything stolen. They weren't worried about us, or you, or Bullet. In fact they didn't ask if any of us were okay. They just ordered us to go to bed. Instead, after they left, we brought out all the remaining vegetables, and made soup."

"We better go back," said Hazel as she shivered from the cold. "I'm scared they'll hurt us if they find us gone."

"We'll be back at sun-up," said Sadie. "I know

they won't be awake until at least noon."

"We'll bring you some breakfast," added Willy.

"I'm going to tie three towels around Bullet's shoulder," said Junior. "You might fall asleep. When we come back in the morning, we'll ask the town vet to come back with us."

When Junior finished binding the towels around Bullet's shoulder, Lucy thanked him. The four children put the scarves back over their faces, put their heads down, and holding hands, hurried back to the apartment.

Chapter Twenty

The letters

*"Be not deceived; God is not mocked: for
whatsoever a man soweth, that shall he also reap."*
Galatians 6:7

Thursday morning
December 23, 1954
Jerilyn and Christopher both awakened around five o'clock, unable to go back to sleep. As they did most mornings of their married lives, they prayed together as soon as they both awakened. Then they checked on their children. They first opened the door to Lily's room and she was still asleep.

They opened the door to Ken's room and he, too, was still asleep. However, when they opened the door to Carrie Emeline's room she was sitting up in bed reading. Carrie Emeline loved the Nancy Drew Mystery stories and was reading the latest book in the series, *The Scarlet Slipper Mystery.*

"Good morning, honey. Why are you awake so early?" Jerilyn asked, as she and Christopher walked over to her and sat on the edge of the bed. "Is it such a good book that you couldn't put it down?"

"It's a good book, but that's not why. In fact I'm not concentrating, so I may as well quit reading and get dressed."

"What's the matter, honey?" asked Jerilyn.

"I was thinking about Lucy and wondering how she was faring at her aunt and uncle's apartment. Do you think she's happy?"

Christopher answered for Jerilyn as he patted Carrie Emeline's hand. "I'm not going to lie to you, honey. Your mom and I are concerned, too." He and Jerilyn both agreed from the day they married that they would not tell untruths to any of their children. They believed honesty flowed in both directions, and they expected the children to be honest with them, also.

Jerilyn said, "You know what happened when your father and I were there on Tuesday."

Carrie Emeline nodded.

"Well, yesterday we went to see Judge James. He agreed the family situation needed assessing. He signed papers to request a social worker from Warren County to visit the family, and to ensure the safety of not just Lucy, but her four cousins, too. Hopefully, the social worker will be able to go today."

"It's been snowing all night," said Carrie Emeline. "I had the radio on earlier and it was reported as a blizzard. Will you and Daddy even be able to get through to Bowling Green?"

"I think so, honey. We'll be very careful. We're going to get the groceries after breakfast and head down the road. Some other cars and trucks have probably already begun leaving us some tracks in the snow ... and the snow has let up."

Jerilyn looked around the room and saw a Bible on the dresser. "Isn't that Lucy's mama's Bible?" she asked.

"Yes, it is," answered Carrie Emeline. "Lucy forgot to take it with her. She was depressed Monday morning and it probably slipped her mind. Maybe you can take it today. Even though she has Bullet, her mama's Bible might give her extra comfort."

"That's a good idea. We'll take it to her this morning," said Jerilyn, as she rose from the bed and picked up the Bible. "We'll see you for breakfast at seven."

Jerilyn made the coffee and joined Christopher in the living room with two steaming cups. She set the cups on the coffee table, and he picked up Lucy's mama's Bible and riffled the pages. He stopped and turned back. There were some papers inserted inside.

Jerilyn sat down on the sofa beside him. "What is it?"

"I'm not sure," he said as he removed the papers. The first page he opened was The Certificate of Baptism for Rose Clark, from the Methodist Church on State Street, dated August 1, 1954. The other thin papers were folded over and the outside of the folded paper was written:

READ THIS LETTER FIRST

From Rose Clark
To: Mr. and Mrs. Christopher Wright
Christmas Hotel
Franklin, Kentucky

They looked at each other puzzled. "Why would Rose write to us?" asked Jerilyn. "How would she even know us?"

"I suppose we're about to find out." He unfolded several pages of paper and read aloud.

"*November 30, 1954.*"

He stopped a moment. "Jerilyn, Lucy's mother wrote this letter the day before she died." He then continued reading aloud.

Dear Mr. and Mrs. Wright,
You don't know me, but I have something to

tell you. Actually, I have something to confess. I hope you can forgive me for what I'm about to say. I anticipate that I'm dying, and I hope you receive these letters soon after I expire.

First I want to tell you a story about what happened eight years ago. On Thanksgiving Day, 1946, my beloved husband Leonard died from tuberculosis. We had been married for only one year. We met in high school and fell in love.

We planned to marry in 1942 when we were graduated, but Leonard joined the army to serve in the war instead. I was so proud of him and loved him so much. While he was in the war I went through nurses' training, and I became a registered nurse in April, 1945.

Leonard arrived back home in late May, 1945, after the war ended in Europe, and we married in Nashville in June. It was the happiest day of my life. We both wanted a family as soon as possible. We lived in a small apartment near Protestant Hospital where I worked. Leonard also found work at the hospital as a patient transporter. I became pregnant with our first child early in March, 1946. I continued to work. I planned to work as long as I possibly could. We hoped to save our money and buy a home by the summer of 1947.

Then Leonard became ill and he tested positive for tuberculosis. Now, instead of working at Protestant Hospital in Nashville, he became a patient in the ward for tuberculosis patients. I was tested, but my test was negative. I could not even visit Leonard. As I said earlier, he died on Thanksgiving Day. I buried him two days later.

I was devastated. I had trouble getting up in the morning and I had to force myself to eat. I knew our baby was due soon, and I needed to take care of myself, but each day was a struggle.

Four days after I buried Leonard, our daughter Lucille Grace Clark was born on December first. She was beautiful, and I now had someone for whom to live. Since I worked as a nurse at Protestant Hospital, I had special privileges to see my daughter whenever I wanted. My room was on the same floor as the nursery and I spent much of my time in the nursery holding her. The day after she was born, I detected something not right. I discussed my suspicion with the pediatrician, and Lucille Grace was thoroughly checked.

Although I tested negative for tuberculosis, it was possible Lucille Grace may have been infected by her father while she was still in the womb. She was scheduled the next day for the test, but she died early in the morning of December third.

At that, Christopher stopped reading and looked at Jerilyn. Jerilyn returned the stare and said in a daze, "Well then ... who is Lucy?"

"I don't know." Christopher returned to reading the letter almost robotically.

I left the hospital on the morning of December third and watched the next day as my sweet Lucille Grace was buried next to Leonard at the Nashville City Cemetery. My husband and now my daughter were dead. On December sixth, I resumed my duties at Protestant Hospital, but not with the enthusiasm I had before Leonard's illness and death. With our child now dead, I wondered why I was alive. I contemplated suicide, but I was told as a young girl that I would go to Hell. I was not a Christian at the time, but I believed in Hell.

Then on Christmas Eve, 1946, I was the nurse on duty in the nursery. As babies were born, I took care of them. At 8:51 that evening a baby girl was born and placed in the nursery. Her tag said "Wright – baby girl," and I overheard her parents the next morning say her name would be Lydia Grace, named for their beloved friend. My heart quickened. It sounded so much like my little Lucille Grace.

Christopher stopped reading. He was too choked up to continue. He heard Jerilyn sob and watched as big tears flowed down her cheeks. She couldn't speak either, and sobbed uncontrollably. Christopher laid the letter on the table and wrapped his arms around Jerilyn. They cried together for the eight years they had lost with their daughter. At least they now knew where she was and that she was alive. They no longer wondered what happened to her.

Christopher finally released Jerilyn. "We have to finish the letter," he said hoarsely. He picked it up and continued reading.

As the parents walked back to the mother's room, I studied the baby girl. She even resembled Lucille Grace with her ringlets of brown curls. It was Christmas morning. I looked around and nobody was watching. I didn't think ... I just reacted. I snatched the baby from her hospital bed unit and ran out of the nursery. My coat hung in the closet behind the nursery. I put it on and wrapped the baby inside my coat. I grabbed some bottles, formula and diapers, and I rushed home to my apartment.

As soon as I arrived home I placed the baby on the bed and packed a suitcase. I had a sister in Bowling Green, Kentucky, and she knew my husband died, but didn't know my baby died, too. I could pass Lydia Grace Wright off as Lucille Grace Clark in another town The hospital would just think I had quit, although I realized they also might suspect I had taken the baby. Because of that, I knew I needed to leave Nashville, and fast. Within sixty minutes I was out of the apartment, and at the L&N Train Station in Nashville. Although it was Christmas morning, the trains were running. I waited about an hour and boarded the train to Bowling Green, Kentucky.

It has not been an easy life and many times I felt regret and wanted to tell you. Lucy and I had our noon meal at Christmas Hotel once or twice a year when I could afford it. I watched you both and knew I had done wrong, but I couldn't take back what I'd done. I loved her and couldn't give her up. I also feared I would go to prison.

Then on Sunday, August first this year, Lucy and I attended church and I came under conviction for all my sins, and I asked the Lord Jesus to come into my heart and save my soul. A peace came over me, and I knew the Lord Jesus had saved me.

Please know that I have loved Lucy and it's going to be hard on me, but I know I need to return her to you. I am presently in bed and ill. I sent Lucy out of the bedroom, and she is now probably asleep on the sofa.

I don't know if I will live, as I probably have pneumonia. As a former registered nurse, I know I have all the symptoms. I just pray Lucy and this letter make their way back to you. Please read the letter to Lucy. I am sure you will know when to tell her, and read Lucy's letter from me to her. By tomorrow I may be absent from this body and present with the Lord.

Please forgive me. Take care of my "Lucy."

Rose Clark

Christopher laid the pages of the letter down a second time. Jerilyn was still crying, and he placed his arm around her shoulder, pulling her body into his.

After a few moments he quietly said, "We can go get her, Jerilyn, and take her away from her horrible aunt and uncle. They're not even her real aunt and uncle. She's *our* daughter. *We're* the next of kin, and this letter is the proof."

Jerilyn pulled a handkerchief from her pocket and blew her nose. "Let's go see Judge James as soon as we tell Lily, Ken, and Carrie Emeline about their sister. But first, I want to hear what Rose wrote to our daughter." Jerilyn spoke her words softly and without malice.

The letter to Lucy was much shorter. Christopher opened the single page and read.

November 30, 1954

Dear Lucy,
I want you to know how much I have loved you. You have been the best daughter a woman could have. I can't tell you how much I have enjoyed having you in my life.

As you know, my husband died before you were born. I was not a very happy woman when he died. You brought joy into my life, but it was the wrong kind of joy. I always knew that, but I really did not know what I needed to do until the day I was saved by Jesus Christ our Lord. You were at church that Sunday on August first this year with me. I knew then that I must tell you the truth. I love you so much that I put it off, but now I am gravely ill.

I don't know if I will live or not. If I do not live, I definitely do not want my sister and her husband raising you. Tonight, before I sent you to get this writing paper, I asked you to forgive me. Of course, you didn't understand what I was talking about. Mr. and Mrs. Wright will explain to you why I need you to forgive me. Please don't be bitter. One should never hold bitterness. The Bible says "Let not your heart be troubled," and I don't want you left with a troubled heart.

Just know that I love you very much. God bless you. I pray you will have a wonderful future, in spite of what I have done. I pray you will find the Lord Jesus at a young age and receive His salvation.

All my love,

"Mama"

*****

Jerilyn and Christopher read the letters to their three children at breakfast. They reacted similarly, as when Christopher and Jerilyn first read them.

"What's the next step?" asked Lily, while wiping the tears from her cheeks.

"Well, we were planning on buying the groceries and driving to Bowling Green first thing this morning," said Christopher. "We also hoped the social worker would be there for the assessment. The situation has now changed. We need to show these letters to Judge James, and hopefully have Sheriff Scott go with us to remove Lucy ... I mean Lydia Grace ... from their home."

"Can we go, too?" asked Ken.

The others joined in with their enthusiasm.

"I don't think that's a good idea," said Jerilyn. "Mr. and Mrs. Smith could be dangerous, and we wouldn't want you children involved in this. I think it will be best if Daddy and I go alone to bring Lydia Grace home, and choose the right time to tell her we're her real family." She looked to Christopher for confirmation.

"I agree completely with your mom. Why don't you three go shopping for a Christmas *and* birthday present for your littlest sister while we're gone? After all, her real birthday is Christmas Eve. Have each gift wrapped accordingly. You can also have a stocking made for her to hang on the mantle at Christmas Hotel. Then, you can stop by the *Blue Rose Bakery* and order a birthday cake.

"Ask them if they can deliver it to Christmas Hotel by the noon meal tomorrow. That should give you something to do while we're in Bowling Green." He reached into his wallet and pulled out folded money and handed it to Lily. He turned to Jerilyn,

"Okay, honey, let's get the ball rolling and bring our youngest child home."

"Yay!" the three children chorused.

*****

Christopher and Jerilyn arrived at the courthouse thirty minutes before court began. Judge James took one look at the letters and signed an order to have Lydia Grace Wright, also known as Lucille Grace Clark, removed from the home of Otto and Eula Mae Smith, and her custody reinstated with her natural parents, Christopher and Jerilyn Wright. Sheriff Scott was called to follow them to the courthouse in Bowling Green.

Since Franklin was in Simpson County, and Bowling Green was in Warren County, Judge James would need an order from a judge in Bowling Green. The phones were working again, so the call was placed and Judge Johnson said he would have the papers ready when they arrived and arrange for a Warren County Sheriff to meet them at the courthouse.

Christopher and Jerilyn decided to forego purchasing the groceries. If the social worker arrived, the four children might be removed too, and then there would be no need for the food. If the children were not removed, they would purchase groceries for them at the market in Bowling Green.

Chapter Twenty-One

Missing!

"Dearly beloved, avenge not yourselves, but rather give place unto wrath: for it is written, Vengeance is mine; I will repay," saith the Lord.
Romans 12:19

Thursday late morning
December 23, 1954
The roads were not as bad as they had anticipated. Even driving slowly, they traveled the twenty-two miles in slightly over an hour. There were already deep tracks in the road to aid in the drive.

Sheriff Scott drove in front of the Wrights with his cruiser lights flashing all the way. They pulled in front of the courthouse and the local sheriff met them out front with the court order. Sheriff Scott and Sheriff Nick Pierce of Warren County shook hands, and Sheriff Scott introduced Sheriff Pierce to Christopher and Jerilyn. In conversation, Christopher and Jerilyn discovered that like Christopher, Sheriff Pierce entered the military after graduation. However, instead of the United

States Army Air Corps that Christopher joined for four years, the sheriff signed up for the United States Navy on the twenty year life program. He attended school in the navy. When he returned home to Bowling Green just two years ago, he ran for sheriff and was elected.

They drove the three vehicles, and parked quietly in front of *Tandy's Billiards*. The two sheriffs kept the cruiser lights off so as not to give advance warning. People on the sidewalk and at Fountain Square Park stopped and stared. It was unusual to see two sheriffs' cars from two different counties in town.

The four walked around back. As they walked, they noticed traces of blood in the snow. They discovered blood on the railing, and on the steps. Christopher nervously hurried up the steps with Jerilyn and the two sheriffs close behind. There was a great deal of blood on the balcony and on the door that led to the hallway. As soon as Christopher opened the exterior door, he stopped. By then Jerilyn and the two sheriffs had caught up with him.

They saw the broken, splintered door and the sheet tacked over the entrance of the Smiths' apartment. "Oh, Heavenly Father, help us all," Christopher prayed aloud, and he grabbed Jerilyn's hand. Christopher and Jerilyn stood in the hallway, afraid to move while the two sheriffs briskly walked to the sheet and pulled it back.

Christopher and Jerilyn cautiously followed them to the entrance of the apartment and they could now see beyond the sheet. There was blood everywhere: all over the floors, furniture and walls. The two sheriffs stood in the doorway and knocked on the door frame. "I am Sheriff Pierce of Warren County, and Sheriff Scott of Simpson County is with me. If there is anyone home, please come forward immediately," Sheriff Pierce announced in a stern voice.

Within thirty seconds, a shirtless Otto and rumpled Eula Mae stumbled out of the bedroom. Otto zipped his pants as he entered and Eula Mae buttoned her sleeveless blouse over the pajama bottoms. They were clearly not accustomed to rising so early, and the two of them appeared to be inebriated.

"Wassa matta, Shuriff?" asked Otto in a slurred voice. He held to the sofa to steady himself.

"What happened here?" asked Sheriff Pierce. "Where did all this blood come from?"

Christopher and Jerilyn stood in the doorway, fearing the answer.

"Oh, ya brung the Wrights wif ya," said Eula Mae. "How ya doin?" she asked as she stumbled to the sofa and plopped down on it, ignoring the sheriff's question.

"I'm going to ask you one more time," said Sheriff Pierce with a sterner voice than before. "What happened here? If I don't get answers right now, I'm taking you both in for questioning."

"Jus a lil accident," said Otto in his slurred speech. "I was cleanin' the revolver an it went off. Boom!" he said with an evil laugh. He belched and laughed even louder.

Jerilyn gasped and Christopher held her around the waist, and hugged her body close to him.

"Where are the children?" demanded Christopher.

"Oh, thar aroun somewars," answered Otto, and loudly belched again. "Ya probly jus missed them out back."

It was now Sheriff Scott's turn to jump in the questioning. "Are you telling us you have five children in your custody and you don't know where any of them are?"

At that question, another person appeared behind them on the threshold. Everyone turned around when she approached. She introduced herself. "I'm Miss Crista Kling from the Warren County Children's Bureau, and I'm here to assess the situation of the children in this family."

"Waddaya mean, missy?" asked Eula Mae, noticeably annoyed as she reached in her pajama pocket, pulled out her tobacco tin, stuck a wad of tobacco in her mouth and began to chew. "We doan need no 'sessment of ar kids. Ya can march yerself back war ya came from." Her anger was clearly apparent to all in the room.

"I take it you two are Otto and Eula Mae Smith, the parents of Otto Eugene Jr., Sadie Ann, William Arnold, and Hazel Louise, and you're the aunt and uncle of Lucille Grace Clark?" asked Miss Kling.

"Yeah, an what's it to ya?" roared Otto, adding some profane language. He steadied himself on the back of the sofa and also pulled a wad of tobacco from his tin, stuffing it in his mouth.

"There are ladies present, so please watch your mouth," demanded Christopher in a strict voice.

"Yeah, Otto, we ladies is present!" Eula Mae mocked, and laughed hysterically.

"How did you two get those bite marks all over your hands and arms?" asked Sheriff Pierce.

"It was thet stupid dog the Wrights brung wif Lucy. He attacked us las night. Broke through thet thar door." Eula Mae pointed to the pieces of door still scattered in the threshold, hallway, and the living room. "We bof bled all over!" She pointed at Otto's and her arm.

"Bullet would not have broken through that door for no reason," said Christopher. "You two must have done something to the children to cause him to do that."

"No, thas not true," insisted Otto. He staggered into the kitchen to get a bucket for him and his wife. He spat in it and when he returned, he held it out for her and she did the same. Jerilyn and Miss Kling cringed. They all turned at the same time, when the sound of footsteps was heard on the back steps. The four Smith children opened the sheet and stepped in.

Eula Mae jumped off the sofa, "Oh, my be-u-tee-ful chilren," she gushed while stumbling toward them. She hugged each of them. "Yer daddy an I was worrit when ya weren't here when we woke up. Are ya'll okay?" she asked, while fawning over each child.

The children stared at her as though she'd lost her mind, and then stepped back, and wrinkled their noses from her foul smelling breath. Junior was the first to speak, "We're fine, Mama – as though you and Daddy even care."

Eula Mae plopped back down on the sofa with her husband, clearly miffed.

"You want to tell us what happened here, son?" Christopher asked softly.

Junior looked at his mama and then his father. "Yes, I'll tell you." Very calmly he revealed the events of the previous evening with the help of his siblings. At one point when Otto yelled, "Thet thar's a lie!" Sheriff Pierce told him to be quiet and have a seat by his wife. When he came to the part regarding what his mama had done to Lucy, Eula Mae jumped off the sofa and hit her son in the stomach with her fist. She snarled at him, "Yer lyin' ta these people. I didn't do a thing yer sayin'!"

Sheriff Pierce snatched her away from her son and pushed her back on the sofa. "If either of you get up again, I'm cuffing you both!" he threatened.

When Jerilyn heard how her daughter had been hit and dragged across the floor by her hair, she turned to Christopher and began to cry softly. Christopher held her close to him and rubbed the back of her head.

When Junior finished the story, Christopher asked, "Did Lucy's lip stop bleeding?"

"I believe so, sir, but I can't be certain. It appeared to have stopped bleeding when we checked on her about one o'clock this morning. Bullet was still bleeding, though, and breathing hard. When we left them for the remainder of the night, Lucy was still applying pressure where we wrapped towels around the wound." He paused, and then added, "Bullet lost a lot of blood, Mr. Wright."

"Did you see them after one o'clock?" asked Jerilyn.

Sadie answered this time, "No, ma'am. We

promised to bring food this morning, but when we arrived at the igloo, they were both gone. At first we thought the igloo had drifting snow on it from the blizzard, and we just didn't find it at first. When we finally found it, Lucy and Bullet weren't inside. There was a trail of blood and paw prints leading into the woods. We followed the trail until the snow drifted over it, and the tracks were gone. We've been out looking for them since about seven o'clock this morning."

"We tried to call you last night, *and* Sheriff Scott, but the telephone lines weren't working," said Junior. "We're sorry, sir. We did everything we could for them."

"It's okay, Junior," said Christopher, while patting Junior's shoulder. "We know you all did what you could. You acted like the exceptional children that you are."

"Thank you, sir," and the four children blushed from the praise they normally did not receive.

"'Ceptional ... phooey!" Eula Mae snarled, her lip curling. "Yer all worthless. Jus lookit whut ya jus said about yer lovin' parents. Lies!"

The four children hung their heads. "Don't listen to them!" Jerilyn demanded, looking at the Smiths' in disgust. "You are *not* worthless. I'm sorry you had to spend your young lives around these people, but we don't believe them. Mr. Wright and I appreciate you very much. Let me see your head, Junior. Did you put anything on that?"

"There was a small amount of hydrogen peroxide that Sadie found in Aunt Rose's medicine cabinet. Sadie washed my head and put the hydrogen peroxide on me late last night."

"You're a smart girl, Sadie." Jerilyn smiled and nodded.

Sadie blushed again from the approval. "Thank you, Mrs. Wright."

"Well, I've heard enough," Miss Kling announced abruptly. "I have assessed this family situation, Sheriff Pierce, and I am removing these four children from the custody of their parents Otto and Eula Mae Smith, and their niece Miss Lucille Grace Clark, as soon as we find her. Do you have any objections, Mr. or Mrs. Smith?"

"None at'll," said Otto as he spat into the bucket.

"Me neither. Take em. I doan wunta see their sorry lyin' faces ever agin!" said Eula Mae.

Miss Kling had papers prepared in advance, should the assessment come to this result. "These are the papers relinquishing all custody rights to your children and your niece. If that is your desire, you may sign here and here." She pointed at the X for Otto Smith and the X for Eula Mae Smith. She handed them a pen and they each made their mark.

She then snapped several pictures of the kitchen and the living room for further evidence.

"Good riddance to ya'll!" said Otto as he spat again in the bucket.

"They're going to need a temporary residence until we can place them in a more permanent situation," said Miss Kling.

Christopher looked at Jerilyn and she nodded in the affirmative. "We'll provide the temporary care for the children," said Christopher. "Before we leave, will you children please show us where you built the igloo? We—"

"Ya'll kin leave *now*," Otto angrily interrupted.

"Not so fast," said Sheriff Pierce. "You two are both under arrest for the abuse of five children. I don't think many people in this county will be too happy about the shooting of the dog either. I'm following you into the bedroom so that you can put on a shirt, coat, and shoes," he said, pointing at Otto. "And you can pull some pants, a shirt, and a coat on over what you're wearing." He pointed to Eula Mae.

When Sheriff Pierce, Eula Mae, and Otto returned to the front room, Sheriff Scott said to Otto and Eula Mae, "Each of you turn around so I can cuff you."

"Whar ya takin us?" demanded Otto.

"You'll be staying in the Warren County Jail

until your trials." He held out the bucket, "You can both spit the remainder of that tobacco in here. I don't want that stuff in my car."

They reluctantly spat the tobacco into the bucket and turned around for the handcuffing. Miss Kling and the Wrights had already led the children out, so they would not have to watch their parents being cuffed.

Before walking out the door, Christopher stuffed the remainder of Lucy's clothes back in her suitcase and latched it. He brought it with them as they left the room. The four Smith children each stuffed some of their belongings into a pillowcase.

While they all trudged through the snow to the igloo, Christopher told Miss Kling that the paperwork for temporary custody on Lucille Grace Clark wouldn't be necessary, and that the two sheriffs could fill her in later. He did not want to discuss Lucy's true identity in front of the Smith children at this time. Miss Kling said she was returning to the courthouse to file the papers, while the children showed the igloo to Christopher and Jerilyn. They found the blankets and bloody towels, but no Lucy or Bullet.

"That was clever of you children to build this igloo for Lucy and Bullet."

"It was Lucy's idea," said Willy. "She said you taught her, and she knew it was not the perfect shelter, but it would keep her and Bullet from freezing."

Christopher smiled. "Yes, I taught her several days ago. Now I just need to find her. You say you followed the tracks and blood, and then they tapered off?"

"Yes, sir," answered Junior, "but the tracks were only dog tracks. There were no little girl tracks. Come on and we'll show you."

They found the dog tracks. Sure enough, they vanished at the edge of the woods. Snow drifts were everywhere. The blizzard must have covered them.

They walked back toward the car, just as the two sheriffs were putting Otto Smith into Sheriff Pierce's cruiser and Eula Mae in Sheriff Scott's cruiser.

Christopher approached Sheriff Scott, while Jerilyn and the four children stood back a few feet from the cruisers that held Otto and Eula Mae.

"I see you didn't find Lucy and Bullet?" said Sheriff Scott.

"No ... not yet," responded Christopher. "What do we do now?"

"I'm going to put out a radio notice to the neighboring counties on the both of them, and then get together a search party." He looked first at Christopher, and then over toward Jerilyn and the children. "We'll find them. Don't worry. We've called for another deputy sheriff to take these two in for booking. You go home and pray for Lucy and Bullet, have something to eat, and if you like, return later after you get these four children settled. They are shaking from the cold temperatures. I realize you have three children at home who are probably worried. I'll call you when I receive any word or lead on Lucy and her dog."

"I think we'll check Fountain Square Park and then Fairview Cemetery before driving the children back home," said Christopher.

"Good. Sheriff Pierce and I will begin searching the woods now, and the search parties will radio me when they arrive. We'll be in touch with you two as soon as we know more."

*****

Christopher and Jerilyn were not fortunate in finding Lucy after checking both places, so they drove home with the Smith children. They pulled up to the curb out front of their house and turned to the four children. "Well, this is your home for now," said Jerilyn as she watched the four faces gape at the beautiful home in awe. They each stepped from the car and stood side by side at the curb.

"Come on, I want you to meet our three children," said Christopher.

The front door opened before they could reach

it. Lily, Ken, and Carrie Emeline stood in the threshold, smiling. Then they frowned. Finally Lily spoke for them. "We thought you were returning with Lucy ... I mean Lydia Grace." She looked at her siblings. "I think we all share the same confusion."

"Let's go inside and sit down. We have a great deal to update you about," Jerilyn sighed, and shook her head slowly.

They settled in the front room, and Jerilyn watched as Junior, Sadie, Willy, and Hazel stared at the tree in amazement. She saw them take in the many brightly colored packages under the tree, and her mother's heart hurt for them. She knew these children had never had a Christmas, let alone a loving environment in which to live. After what she had witnessed today, she also knew how badly they had been treated in their young lives. The things her children took for granted, these children could only imagine. She also knew the alternative was probably an orphanage. Not many people were willing to adopt children of their ages. She realized they would be split up if anyone was willing to adopt only one of them. This could be the last Christmas they spent together as a family. Although Jerilyn was desperately worried about Lucy, or more accurately, she realized, Lydia Grace, she also had concern for these four children.

Christopher's voice interrupted her thoughts as

he conveyed the events of the past twenty-four hours to their three children, and the Smith children adding details when asked. Jerilyn noticed he did not sugarcoat anything; he simply told them the facts. She agreed that they were old enough to know the truth and she, too, wanted them to hear every bit of the story.

Jerilyn now watched the faces of her three children and the four Smith children. Her girls began to cry when they heard what was done to Lucy, while Ken held the same gaze throughout most of the dissertation by his father. The only change in his expression that Jerilyn observed was when he heard about the striking of Lucy's face and dragging her across the floor by her hair. It was then that he winced.

The four Smith children appeared quite surprised, but pleased for Lucy, when Christopher revealed she was part of the Wright family and not the Smith family. "However, we will find the right time to tell Lucy she is Lydia Grace ... as soon as she's found," Christopher said, as he completed his story.

When he finished, they all sat for a moment in silence. Finally Lily spoke for the children, "What now? Do we sit and wait, or go help look for her?"

"Sheriff Scott promised an update as soon as he knows something," said Christopher. "Let's have prayer for Lucy, and then your mom and I will join the search in Bowling Green. Your mother and I need you to stay here, Lily. I'm sure these children need fed, too."

Lily nodded. "I'll take care of them, Dad."

Jerilyn knew the Smith children were not accustomed to so much prayer, and they hesitated at first, but then politely joined hands with the family as Christopher prayed aloud.

"Dear Heavenly Father, We are gathered here to ask for Thy divine assistance in finding our lost family member Lucy ... Lydia Grace. We don't know where she is but we know that Thou in Thy infinite wisdom dost know. Please keep her safe as the sheriffs and the search party look for her. Please give us strength as we wait for the news. In the name of Jesus we pray... amen."

Jerilyn, Lily, Ken, and Carrie Emeline echoed their amens, and the Smith children softly said amen.

Jerilyn understood it was probably only the second time the Smith children had prayed together. She wondered if they had ever been to church. She made a mental note to change that this Christmas. They always held a candlelight service in the chapel at Christmas Hotel each year. This year they would invite these four children to join them.

Chapter Twenty-Two

Christmas Hotel Chapel

"Behold, I send an Angel before thee, to keep thee in the way, and to bring thee into the place which I have prepared."
Exodus 23:20

Thursday afternoon
December 23, 1954
Before returning to Bowling Green to join the search for Lydia Grace, Christopher and Jerilyn asked Lily to not only prepare food for the Smith children, but to get them settled in their home for the time being. Lily had her own room, and Ken already had two sets of bunk beds in his room for the many sleepovers of his friends. Therefore it was no problem to have Junior and Willy share his room. Sadie and Hazel would use the double bed in the guest room, because as soon as Lydia Grace was found, she would probably want to continue to sleep in the other twin bed in Carrie Emeline's room.

Christopher and Jerilyn discussed the guardianship of the Smith children with Lily. "We need for you to watch over them while we're gone," said Christopher. "I know it's a big responsibility, but I think you're up for it."

Jerilyn smiled at her daughter. "Especially if you plan to be a teacher."

"I'm sure we'll be just fine, and I have Ken and Carrie Emeline to help me. You two go quickly and find my littlest sister," Lily said, and kissed her parents goodbye. "I'll be praying she's found and soon."

They sat in the station wagon, but Jerilyn wondered why Christopher did not start the car. "I have a strong quickening in my soul to go to the chapel at Christmas Hotel to pray," he explained. "Maybe I'm having this feeling because in the Christmas Hotel chapel is where you and I have found our miracles and peace. I just feel an urgency that we need to go there and pray."

Jerilyn looked into Christopher's eyes. She learned a long time ago that when Christopher had these feelings, they were from the Lord. Although she also loved the Lord, and was a Christian, she knew Christopher had a closeness that was beyond compare. When he was called to preach, he knew he could not refuse. He knew preaching was his destiny. Jerilyn never questioned him, but she simply said, "I agree, Christopher."

He started the car and they drove to Christmas Hotel and parked on the East Cedar Street side.

They entered the hotel and nodded to Christopher's manager on duty, Patrick Mullins. They both noticed the newest Christmas stocking their children had hung for Lydia Grace.

Jerilyn looked at Christopher and smiled, but her eyes glistened with tears.

Jerilyn looked at Christopher and smiled, and her eyes glistened with tears.

"We'll find her, honey," he said comfortingly, and hugged her to his side. "Let's go pray."

When they entered the chapel, they knew something was amiss. No lights were on, one candle was lit, but they saw no one. They knew a candle would never be left lit. Mr. Mullins would have checked. They held hands and walked to the front row of pews to kneel at the altar. As they reached the front row of pews they saw a bundle lying on the first pew. As they walked toward it for closer examination, they saw it was a small child wrapped in a patchwork quilt. The light was dim, but they could make out that the child was a girl by the long curly hair. Jerilyn gently moved the curls from the child's face, and removed the cold towels that contained melting ice. The child was Lydia Grace.

She looked at Christopher, placed her hand over her mouth, and whispered, "Oh, Christopher. She's here. She's alive." Jerilyn muffled the sobs that escaped from her throat.

"Watch over her, Jerilyn," he said, as he hurried out of the chapel.

He walked up to Mr. Mullins. "Did you see a small child or anyone else come into the chapel?"

"No, sir," said the morning duty manager.

Mr. Mullen's eyes widened in surprise.

"There's a little girl asleep on the front pew in the chapel, and no one saw her or knows how she got there?"

"I'm sorry, Mr. Wright. If I'd known a child was in there or someone left her there, I would have notified you. I've been on duty since six o'clock this morning and I've seen no one enter the chapel."

"It's okay, Patrick. I didn't mean to sound as though I was interrogating you. I was also concerned because a candle was lit and left unattended. The child happens to be the child that was missing from Bowling Green, and who also happens to be the kidnapped daughter of Mrs. Wright and myself from eight years ago."

Christopher saw the confusion on Patrick Mullen's face.

Christopher chuckled. "I'll explain later, Patrick. I thank God we found her. I'll take it from here. I have lots of people to notify."

He hurried back into the chapel. His eyes teared as he watched Jerilyn crying while holding and rocking their daughter.

*****

Eight hours earlier, an old horse-drawn farm wagon pulled up at the curb on the square in Bowling Green. Mr. Gabe set the parking brake and stepped down from the wagon, pulling a patchwork quilt from under the seat. He wrapped the reins of the horse around a light pole, and walked toward the igloo in the field. He stood back about five feet from the entrance, and Bullet slowly rose when he saw Mr. Gabe.

Mr. Gabe watched as Bullet licked the face of the sleeping Lucy. Bullet then looked directly into Mr. Gabe's eyes before he turned and slowly hobbled toward the woods, leaving a bloody trail in the snow. Bullet had been Lucy's guardian as long as possible, and now it was Mr. Gabe's turn. Mr. Gabe looked to the heavens and sighed. "The mission of Miss Lucy's prayer on December first is nearly accomplished, Lord."

He gently lifted Lucy from the igloo and laid her in the quilt. Her lip was still bleeding slightly and there was a huge bruise around her right cheek, along with a cut in her flesh around the eye. Her whole face was swollen. He carefully wrapped Lucy in the quilt, lifted his bundle to his shoulder and walked back to the wagon. He gently laid her on the passenger area of the bench seat, then untied the reins from the light pole, and hoisted himself into the driver's seat. After releasing the parking brake, he made a clicking sound to Ol' Bob, and slapped the reins on the horse's back. Lucy did not stir the entire ride to Mr. Gabe's cabin.

The horse trotted down the lane back to the pristine cabin. "Whoa, Ol Bob." Mr. Gabe set the parking brake and jumped down. After freeing Ol' Bob from his harness and setting him loose to roam in the paddock, Mr. Gabe gently picked up his sleeping bundle. He carried Lucy through the front door and laid her on the sofa. Wetting a washcloth, he added some soap, and gently washed her face. Opening the cupboard in the kitchen, he located the antiseptic and cotton, and dabbed at the cuts on her face. Even when he bandaged the cuts, Lucy remained asleep. He built the fire and made the breakfast, just as he had on December second when he first met Lucy.

Lucy finally awakened and stumbled into the kitchen just as he set the food on the table. She looked around, completely confused. "Mr. Gabe ... how did I get here? Where's Bullet? And the house looks like it did when I was here with you before. I'm so mixed up."

"Sit down, child. Let's have breakfast, and I'll explain about Bullet as best as I can."

After they prayed, Mr. Gabe watched while Lucy ate. She was obviously famished. When she finished, he spoke softly to her. "I'm going to put ice in some towels for your face. It will help the swelling." He chipped off some ice from the block in the icebox, and wrapped the ice in two kitchen towels. "Let's go into the front room and we'll talk." He took her hand and led her to the sofa. He held the ice pack to her face.

She asked him again, "Where's Bullet?"

He saw the nearly frantic expression on her face. "I won't lie to you, Lucy. Bullet was hurt badly. When I found you in the igloo, I saw Bullet was bleeding ... a lot. I watched Bullet lick your face and walk away. I'm sorry, child, I know how much he meant to you. I know this is hard for you, especially so soon after your mama's death." He sighed and looked into her tearful eyes. "You have had a lot of hurt for such a young child. Life is hard, but, Lucy, I promise God loves you and He has a plan. In fact He's been watching over you all the days of your life since you were born."

"Is Bullet ... dead, too? Like my ... mama?" She struggled with the words.

"I don't know for certain, child, but I do know that when animals are seriously wounded, they usually go off by themselves. I think when Bullet licked your face he was telling you goodbye. I want you to know that he didn't leave you until I arrived. He was guarding you until the very end."

Lucy began to cry. "He loved me and protected me, Mr. Gabe. Now I have nobody. He was all I had left. Christmas is coming, but there won't be a Christmas for me this year." Her body heaved with sobs.

He hugged her close. "Yes, you have someone, child. In fact, you have lots of someones. Your life is about to change in an unexpected, but beautiful way. Things are going to be revealed to you that will hurt you at first, but you will later understand. You're going to a family that will love you very much. You're going to have a lovely life. I also promise you there *will* be a Christmas for Lucy this year. "

She looked up into his kind, wrinkled face. "How do you know that?"

He smiled. "I just do, Lucy."

"I'm sleepy again, Mr. Gabe."

"I know, child. It's been a rough night for you. The next time you awaken, your new life will begin."

"Will I see you again?"

"I will always be near. You prayed to the Baby Jesus on December first for Him to protect you. That's what Bullet and I have done. Your new family will take over where we left off. You'll be fine, Lucy. I promise." He patted her arm reassuringly.

At that statement her eyes closed. She leaned into Mr. Gabe and fell asleep. He laid her gently down on her side, and he repositioned the ice pack on her cheek. He walked outside and re-hitched Ol' Bob to the wagon. Walking back into the cabin one last time, he bundled Lucy in the quilt, took a final look at the cabin, and smiled at the picture of the lovely lady above the fireplace.

Placing Lucy on the wagon's seat, he hopped aboard. Releasing the parking brake, he called to the horse. "Giddap, Ol' Bob," and the wagon headed down the road to Christmas Hotel.

Mr. Gabe again parked on East Cedar Street and carried the sleeping Lucy inside. He did not see the manager on duty, so he headed to the chapel and placed Lucy on the front pew with the ice pack resting on her cheek. He lit a candle.

"I am finished, Lord Jesus. I have done what Thou asked. She is now under the protection of Christmas Hotel until her parents arrive." He said a prayer over Lucy, and slipped unnoticed from the building.

Chapter Twenty-Three

Revelations

*"The angel of the LORD encampeth round about
them that fear him, and delivereth them."*
Psalm 34:7

Thursday afternoon
December 23, 1954
"Did you see Mr. Gabe?" asked Lucy.

Jerilyn looked at Christopher. "No. Did you,
Christopher?"

"No, I didn't. In fact, I just checked with Mr.
Mullins, and he saw no one enter Christmas Hotel
with Lucy." He then asked Lucy, "Are you saying
Mr. Gabe brought you here?"

"Yes, sir." She then told them everything that
had happened. When she told them what Mr. Gabe
said about Bullet leaving the igloo, she buried her
head into Jerilyn's breast and cried. "Bullet loved
me and protected me. I loved him, too. I miss him
so much."

Jerilyn stroked her head and kissed her on the
cheek. "I know, honey. It's hard to lose someone,
but Mr. Christopher and I want you to know we
love you, and we will protect you. You won't have to

ever see your aunt and uncle again. In fact, if it's okay with you, you are coming home to live with us forever."

Lucy looked at Jerilyn in amazement. "You both want me?" Her gaze darted from one to the other.

Christopher answered her. "Yes, honey, we want you very much. We have so much to tell you. We're going to reveal things to you that will hurt you at first, but you will later understand."

"That's what Mr. Gabe said." Lucy scrunched her face in bewilderment. "He also said he would be near. Does that mean I'll never see him again?"

Christopher looked to Jerilyn and then answered, "I don't know, but I think you've been watched over for a long time. You're a precious little girl. However, now, with the Lord's help we're going to take care of you. We love you, and so do Lily, Ken, and Carrie Emeline. We'll do our best to make certain your life is filled with happiness. Are you ready to go home now?"

Lucy smiled. "Yes. I'm ready to go home."

*****

Before they left Christmas Hotel, they stopped at the front desk to call the sheriff's office in Bowling Green. The dispatch officer answered the phone. Christopher explained the situation and asked him to relay the information to Sheriffs Scott and Pierce. Christopher and Jerilyn returned to the car with Lydia Grace and headed home.

When they entered, seven children greeted them with whoops and hollers. Even Daisy rose from the warm hearth to greet Lucy.

After the children settled down, Christopher said, "I realize how excited all of you are to see Lucy, but we need to speak to her privately." Christopher then turned to Lily and whispered, "Did you take care of the gifts?"

"All taken care of, Dad," answered Lily with a thumbs-up.

"Then if you children don't mind, I'd like for you to go to your rooms or outside while we talk to Lucy."

The children conversed, and then put on their coats and headed outdoors.

Jerilyn wrapped some more ice in towels for Lucy's face. Christopher retrieved Rose Clark's Bible, and then he and Jerilyn settled on the sofa and asked Lucy to join them. Christopher patted the space between them while Jerilyn handed the ice wrapped in the towel to Lucy to hold to her cheek.

"Lucy, I know you recognize this Bible that belonged to your mama," Christopher began, and Lucy nodded.

Jerilyn continued the conversation. "We found a couple of letters in the Bible. You told me that you remembered your mama asking you to bring her a paper and pen the night before she died."

"Yes," said Lucy. "She told me she needed to write something. She asked me to forgive her, too."

Jerilyn responded with, "I know, honey. What she wrote that night, we found in her Bible. I think she was hoping the letters would be found quickly and mailed to us. We didn't find them until early this morning." She nodded to Christopher.

"I'm going to read the letter to you that your mama wrote you," said Christopher.

Jerilyn observed the different expressions of happiness and puzzlement on Lucy's face while Christopher read.

When Christopher was finished, he asked, "Do you have any questions so far, Lucy?"

"What does Mama mean I shouldn't hold bitterness? What does she mean in spite of what she's done? Did Mama think I would be mad at her for dying?"

Jerilyn placed her arm around Lucy. "No, honey, that's not what she meant. She also wrote another letter. I think Mr. Christopher and I will just tell you the gist of the other letter. It's much longer and a little confusing for you now. You'll understand the letter better when you're older." She nodded to Christopher.

Christopher sighed and began. "That same

night, she wrote a letter to Mrs. Jerilyn and me."

Now Lucy was really confused. "I don't understand. Mama didn't know you and Mrs. Jerilyn."

Jerilyn said softly, "In a way she did, Lucy. Mr. Christopher is going to tell you how she knew us."

Christopher took a deep breath. "Your mama believed she was dying, and she wanted to be sure you were taken care of. She also wanted to right a wrong she committed eight years ago. She explained in the letter how her husband died on Thanksgiving just before her beautiful baby girl Lucille Grace Clark was born."

Lucy smiled with this statement.

"She said in her letter she had become a registered nurse, while her husband was off fighting the war. After her husband returned from the war, they became pregnant with you. Her husband died shortly before her baby was born. Because of her nurse's training, she was able to detect that something was wrong with her baby. She discussed her suspicion with the pediatrician, and Lucille Grace was thoroughly checked. She thought her baby might have been infected while still in her tummy by the same illness from which her husband died. The baby was scheduled the next day for the test, but the baby...." Christopher struggled to complete the sentence and he looked to

Jerilyn for support. She nodded for him to continue.

"The baby died early in the morning of December third."

They watched Lucy's face as she processed the information.

When she finally spoke, it was with hesitation. "I ... don't ... understand," she said with eyebrows knitted together and a frown on her face. She tilted her head. "That can't be. I'm not dead. I'm ... sitting right here. Why ... why would Mama write that to you?"

Christopher continued, while Jerilyn kept her arm around Lucy. "Remember, I said your mama wanted to right a wrong she committed eight years ago?"

Lucy nodded, but she retained the perplexed look on her face.

"Well, your mama went into a deep depression after burying her daughter so soon after burying her husband, but she did return to her nursing duties at Protestant Hospital in Nashville. On the evening of Christmas Eve, 1946, a baby girl was born. The next morning she heard the parents of the baby discuss naming her Lydia Grace, after a dear friend. Your mama thought the baby even resembled her Lucy who had died. Both babies had curly brown hair."

He paused, and watched the expression on Lucy's face. Lucy was still mulling over this last bit of information. She was a smart little girl and her thoughts clearly began to run together. She dropped the towel and the ice slid across the floor. Finally she blurted, "*I'm* that little girl. My mama took me. She *stole* someone's baby, didn't she?" She stopped and began breathing hard. Tears streamed down her cheeks. "How could she do that? I thought *I* was her little girl. I thought she was my mama. I ... loved her! She was ... a ... a ... *bad* person!"

Jerilyn pulled her into her arms and let her cry it out. Christopher handed Jerilyn a handkerchief for Lucy. The crying began to subside, and Lucy started hiccupping. Jerilyn held out the handkerchief for her and the little girl accepted it. When she finished wiping her eyes and blowing her nose, Jerilyn spoke softly to her.

"Rose Clark, the woman you knew as your mama, was a very troubled person. She couldn't handle the fact that her two loved ones were dead – the baby and her husband. She thought about taking her own life, but she was smart enough to know she would go to Hell. Last August, when she received the Lord's salvation, she realized she needed to reveal to your real parents that you were alive and well. She knew she had done wrong. She'd grown to love you so much and it was difficult. The night before she died, she suspected it might be her last night on earth." Jerilyn stopped and looked into Lucy's eyes.

Lucy returned the stare, and then she asked, "Who ... am I? Why did she write the letters to you?"

Christopher answered gently. "She wrote the letters to us, because *you* are *our* daughter Lydia Grace Wright. *You* are our baby that she took from the nursery that night." Christopher and Jerilyn's eyes now welled up with tears. "You're the baby sister to Lily, Ken and Carrie Emeline. They know the truth, and they're thrilled to have you home. How ... how do you feel about all this information?"

Christopher and Jerilyn watched their daughter's face change from sadness to happiness. After a moment she spoke. "All I can think of right now is that I'm with a family who loves me. You're not just *any* family, you're my *real* family. Just think, I'll never have to go back to my aunt and my uncle ... those two horrid people." She turned to Christopher and placed her arms around him, and he hugged her in return. "I'm fine. I'm *glad* you're my daddy. I've always wanted a Daddy." She then turned to Jerilyn. "I already love you both." They watched her face change to surprise. "I just thought of something. My real birthday is tomorrow and not

December first!"

Christopher and Jerilyn laughed. "Yes, it is, honey," said Jerilyn lovingly, while smoothing her daughter's hair. "You now have a new birthday."

"I can't wait to see my sisters and brother." Then her face saddened. "Junior, Sadie, Willy, and Hazel ... they're not my cousins. What will happen to them?"

"Don't be frightened for them, honey," Jerilyn answered. "They're staying with us temporarily, until the courts make that decision. I have a feeling their future will be much better. They won't be returning to their parents. You don't have to worry about that. They also know you're not their cousin, and they're happy for you. They really do love you."

"I love them, too, now. I used to be scared of them. They were nicer to me after they met you and...." Her voice trailed away. "I don't know what to call you two. If I say Mama, I'll think of ... Rose Clark."

Jerilyn answered, and said, "Our children called us Mommy and Daddy at your age. Lately, though, I seem to have become Mom."

"May I call you Mommy and Daddy?"

"Sweetheart, we would be honored to be addressed as Mommy and Daddy by you," said Jerilyn.

"I realize you have been Lucy Clark for the past

eight years," broached Christopher. "Your mommy and I have talked about how to discuss your name with you. We would like to call you Lydia Grace ... but only if that's what you want. We don't want you to feel like we are forcing a new name on you. You've already had a lot of changes to face. If—"

She interrupted Christopher. "I want you to call me Lydia Grace. That's my real name. I never was Lucy. Lucy was a baby that died."

"We want you to be sure," continued Christopher. "If at any point you want to change your mind, and prefer us to call you Lucy, will you promise to come and tell us that you've changed your mind?"

"Yes, Daddy, I promise."

"We love you ... Lydia Grace. Welcome home, our darling little girl," and they each hugged Lydia Grace.

Chapter Twenty-Four

Family Love

*"Beloved, let us love one another: for love is of
God; and every one that loveth is born of God,
and knoweth God."*
1 John 4:7

Friday morning
December 24, 1954
It was Christmas Eve, but also the true birthday of
Lydia Grace Wright. She was again sharing Carrie
Emeline's bedroom, and Carrie Emeline had to
awaken her that morning. Lydia Grace was finally
sleeping peacefully. Her ordeal with Otto and Eula
Mae was over and she no longer had to worry about
returning to them.

Carrie Emeline shook her and bounced on the
bed. "Wake up, sleepy head!"

Lydia Grace finally aroused, stretched her arms,
and smiled at her sister.

"You know the best part of you being my sister
is that I'm no longer the younger sister to Lily. *You*
are now the youngest girl in the family." She began
to tickle Lydia Grace and they both laughed.

Then Carrie Emeline became serious. "I was too young to really remember when you were born, but Lily does. She said our parents were really upset when their baby girl went missing. As you know, Lily's real mom died when Lily was born, and Ken's and my real dad died in the war. You were Mom and Dad's only child together. Around us, they tried not to show how upset they were. Lily said that the stress from losing you was probably why Mom had the two miscarriages. Lily knew about you being stolen. She secretly told us when we were old enough to understand, and I'm glad she did. I love you, Lydia Grace." Carrie Emeline leaned forward and pulled Lydia Grace into a hug.

Lydia Grace returned the embrace. "I love you, too, Carrie Emeline. Thank you for being my friend even before you knew I was your sister."

"You are most welcome, little sister. Now, let's get dressed and head downstairs. We always have a special breakfast on our birthdays. Since it's your birthday, and our first birthday with you, I'll predict a super special breakfast this morning. Are you hungry?"

Lydia Grace took a deep breath through her nose. "I can smell lots of different smells, and I'm starved!"

"Well, let's get dressed and head downstairs. I'll brush your hair first."

Fifteen minutes later, all the Wright family and the Smith children were assembled in the kitchen, savoring the wonderful scents. "Lydia Grace, we weren't sure what your favorites were, so we prepared everything we could think of," said Jerilyn, smiling. "The last time we did this, you were whisked away too soon. As you know, we always make the favorite breakfast of each family member on his or her birthday."

"Carrie Emeline told me," said Lucy, jumping up and down in excitement. "I smelled all sorts of different kinds of food cooking."

"Well, we've combined all the favorites for you, so you can decide what your favorite is for your future birthdays."

They sat down to a breakfast of blueberry and strawberry pancakes, chocolate muffins, omelets made with ham, cheese, and tomatoes, grits, link sausage, bacon, and biscuits and gravy. Earlier, Lily and Sadie had set the table with the best silverware, a poinsettia centerpiece, and two tapered candles in silver candlestick holders. Christopher, Jerilyn, Lily, and the twins carried the steaming dishes into the dining room. "It's not often that we use ten of our twelve chairs around this table," said Jerilyn with a chuckle. "It's wonderful filling so many seats with mostly children!"

"I agree," said Christopher. "Before we sit, let's

all hold hands, thank the Lord, and ask His blessing.

"Dear Heavenly Father, we are gathered here today, and we thank Thee for the pleasing food Thou hath provided for the nourishment of our bodies. We are grateful and thankful that Thou has safely returned our youngest child home to us. When Lydia Grace was missing, only Thou knew what an emptiness was created in our family. We ask for Thy guidance to help us raise Lydia Grace properly. We also thank Thou for allowing us to temporarily care for Junior, Sadie, Willy, and Hazel. They are a blessing to have in our home. We ask Thee to aid us in finding a loving home that will want all four children, and parents to guide them to know Thou. We ask all this in the name of Thy Son Jesus. Amen."

The family added their amens. Tears appeared on the faces of all the children. The boys tried to conceal the reaction by looking down and quickly wiping their eyes.

"Let's sit down and enjoy this delightful feast," said Christopher.

"*Yay!*" the children shouted in unison.

After breakfast, Jerilyn called their beloved friend Dr. Beasley to stop by. He examined Lydia Grace, Junior, and Willy. He pronounced the injuries as not serious, and to continue applying the ice every three hours, and ten minutes each interval for one more day on Lydia Grace's face to reduce the swelling.

*****

After Dr. Beasley left, Jerilyn, Lily, and Carrie Emeline volunteered to clean up the kitchen, while Christopher and the remaining children went out back to play in the snow. The igloos were still there along with the two snowmen. Lydia Grace stood and stared at the igloos and a tear slid down her face. Sadie walked over to her and placed her arm around her. "You miss Bullet, don't you, Lydia Grace?"

Lydia Grace bowed her head, nodded her head in the affirmative, and her shoulders began to shake. Sadie pulled her close and held her while she cried. "He was my friend, and he died saving me. I don't know what I did to deserve his love. That first morning when the woman I thought was my mama died, and Uncle ... I mean Mr. and Mrs. Smith made me leave, it was so cold. Later that first night, Bullet came from nowhere and he kept me warm at the fountain. From then on, he was always with me, except when I was in school. He was there protecting me." She stopped a minute and wiped the tears from her cheeks. "I don't want my mommy and my daddy to think Bullet meant more to me than them," she said softly. "I'm also angry with Rose Clark for stealing me. I thought she was my real mama all these years. I loved her, but she was a *bad* woman for what she did."

"I'm having awful feelings about my parents and so are Junior, Willy, and Hazel," said Sadie. "We didn't know there were kind families in the world until we met the Wrights. We thought our family was normal. I do know this though: somehow we're all going to have to learn how to forgive. I think it will be easier for you. You have a wonderful family now. The four of us still don't know what's going to happen to us. I don't know much about God, but the Wrights do. I know they pray and trust God. I think we all need to learn how to do that. I really have a feeling that it will be okay for all of us."

They looked up and saw that the others were waiting and watching. Although Christopher had overheard everything, he tried not to let on to the girls. He just said a prayer in his heart. *We thank Thee, Lord. We thank Thee for allowing Sadie to understand and help Lydia Grace. I couldn't have said it better myself. When the time is right, I now have a way to help Lydia Grace understand why Thou sent Thy Son to us. We thank Thee, Lord.*

Christopher gathered the children, and he and Ken explained how to play backyard tag in the snow. They tracked a big circle around the perimeter of the yard, with an X tracked in the middle of it. He told the children someone would be "It", and the person who was "It" would need to catch anyone and tag them. However, each person needed to stay on the circle path or on the X path. "The person who 'It' tags can't turn around and tag the former 'It' again, but must catch someone else. The person remaining is the winner." Christopher added, "Let's play rock, paper, and scissors until we can determine the first 'It'."

After four rounds of rock, paper, and scissors, Christopher lost, and the six children began running from him on the circle or in the X. They laughed and continued to look around to see where Christopher might be. He eventually tagged Ken first, so Ken began running after another child.

Jerilyn appeared at the back door. "Christopher, please come into the house. I have something important to discuss privately." He entered the mudroom that was just off from the kitchen. He took off his outer clothes and hung them on the wall hooks, and removed his boots and set them on the rug to dry.

Jerilyn looked puzzled. "I just received a telephone call from Darius. He and Barbara are on their way over here. He says they want to speak with us regarding the Smith children."

"Did he give you any indication as to what they

wanted to discuss?"

"No, not really."

"Are Lily and Carrie Emeline still working in the kitchen?"

"Yes."

"Let's you and me go in to the living room. I want to tell you something before Darius and Barbara get here."

After hearing what transpired between Lydia Grace and Sadie, Jerilyn just shook her head sadly. "Christopher, I don't know what is worse for our daughter: the death of Bullet or the betrayal by Rose Clark. We need to pray for the Lord to guide us."

They held hands and when they finished praying, the doorbell rang. Together they answered the door and greeted Darius and Barbara.

"Please come in and have a seat in the living room," said Jerilyn smiling. "May I get you a cup of coffee, a soda, or a glass of water?"

"No, thank you," said Darius. "We're fine, and I don't think this will take long."

They ushered Darius and Barbara to the sofa and sat across from them in the matching fireside chairs. Darius took Barbara's hand and kissed it. Darius looked at Barbara lovingly, and she nodded and smiled. They looked back at Christopher and Jerilyn.

Darius cleared his throat in a slightly self-conscious way. "As you know, Barbara and I have been married for some time. Regrettably, we've not been blessed with children. However, we have now decided there was a reason. As we all know, the Lord does things in His own timing. The night we arrested Otto and Eula Mae Smith, I heard some horrendous things they said in front of their own children, and I've told Barbara about them. I was flabbergasted to hear those two wretched human beings tell their own offspring that they were 'worthless do-nothing' children. I'd heard about parents, such as them, but had never experienced it."

He looked again at Barbara and she smiled. "We're here to ask your permission to foster the four children until we can apply for adoption. If you're in agreement, we'd like to see Judge James before he goes home today. As the temporary guardians, are you willing for us to adopt them? Will you give us your blessing?"

Christopher stood and walked to Darius and shook his hand. "I can't think of better people to become parents than you two! You're an answer to our prayers!" They all stood and the women hugged each other. "When do you plan on taking them?"

"Today, if possible. We need to see the judge and get the signed order to foster them. Then we want to go shopping. Hopefully, you two can give us some advice for Christmas gifts. They probably need clothes, too. How old is each child?"

Jerilyn jumped in to supply this information. "Junior is fourteen, Sadie is thirteen, Willy is twelve, and Hazel is ten. As far as clothes, I think the best people to go shopping with you are Lily and our twins. They will easily be able to gauge the sizes for clothes, and suggest Christmas gifts."

"That sounds like a plan," said Darius. "We'll go now and talk to Judge James, and get the signed custody paper to foster the children. Where would you like to meet?"

"How about we all meet at Christmas Hotel for the noon meal," said Christopher. "We already have a birthday cake that was delivered there to celebrate Lydia Grace's real birthday. You two can celebrate with us. You and our three older children can leave and go shopping with you afterwards. When you're finished, meet us back at our house around five. We can have Lydia Grace open her birthday present before dinner, and then tell the Smith children the good news. Then I'd like to invite all of you to attend the Candlelight Christmas Eve service in the chapel at Christmas Hotel tonight at seven o'clock. We plan on caroling around town for about an hour to end the evening."

Barbara spoke for the first time. "We'd be

delighted to attend the service, as a new family. Thank you both so much. Darius and I have prayed for so long to have a family. I just can't wait."

"Well, I want to warn you," said Christopher, "even when children are raised in a loving home, they will still be imperfect children. With the home environment the Smith children have been raised, you may be acquiring some unruly children."

Darius just laughed. "What better couple to keep them in line but a sheriff, and a church secretary who's also a Sunday school teacher! We're honored to take on the responsibility."

Chapter Twenty-Five

The Long Awaited Children

"And we know that all things work together for good to them that love God, to them who are the called according to his purpose."
Romans 8:28

Friday at Christmas Hotel
December 24, 1954
At noon, the four adults and eight children entered the Christmas Hotel lobby and immediately walked over to the newest stocking hanging from the mantle. Lily touched the red and green stocking that read Lydia Grace. "Lydia Grace, I want you to know that you are now officially part of the Wright family, and we welcome you!"

The family, friends, and Christmas Hotel staff clapped, and Lily hugged and kissed Lydia Grace.

Lily pointed to her stocking and her dad's. "Daddy's stocking and my stocking led the Wright family tradition in 1936 when I was born. Mom's stocking was added in 1941 when she joined the family, and the stockings for Ken and Carrie Emeline were added their first Christmas in 1942. It's been a long eight-year wait to add your stocking. We're all so happy you are finally home, Lydia Grace."

Lily, Ken and Carrie Emeline each hugged Lydia Grace, and everyone applauded again.

Lydia Grace wiped tears of happiness and glanced from one family member to the next. "Thank you all so much. I'm so happy to be home."

The four adults and eight children finished their meal in the dining room, and Lydia Grace was stunned to receive her second birthday cake. Their waiter brought it out and set the cake in front of Lydia Grace with the eight candles lit. "Wow, two cakes this year!"

"Make a wish, Lydia Grace and blow out the candles!" Lily encouraged her littlest sister. "But don't tell us what you wish for."

Lydia Grace closed her eyes and thought for a moment. Taking a big breath, she blew out all the candles with one breath. The waiters joined in along with the dining room guests, as everyone sang "Happy Birthday."

While Jerilyn cut the cake and served it to everyone at the table, Carrie Emeline reached in her pocket and handed Lydia Grace her gift. "Lily, Ken and I picked out your birthday gift."

"I hope you like it," Ken added.

Lydia Grace tore open the wrapping, and she held up the silver bracelet for all to see. Fingering the tiny charms with all the Wright family names engraved, she cried. "That was one of my wishes. I made two wishes. To be happy this Christmas, and I am." She wiped another tear. "I love you all so very much. I hope my other wish comes true, too!"

Jerilyn stood and planted a kiss on her daughter's cheek. "We love you too, Lydia Grace. We couldn't be happier on this very special Christmas Eve."

Following the celebration, the Scotts took their leave with Lily and the twins to go Christmas shopping. Christopher and Jerilyn had informed their three older children earlier what would happen after the noon meal, and they were thrilled and excited for the Smith children.

The Scotts, Lily, and the twins arrived back at the Wright home promptly at five. All twelve settled in the living room, and then Lily hurried upstairs for the second of Lydia Grace's birthday presents. As she descended the staircase, the family and friends began singing "Happy Birthday" again.

Lydia Grace's face lit up with excitement. She clapped her hands with joy as Lily set the big box in front of her. She squealed with excitement. "Another birthday present!"

"Go ahead and unwrap it, honey," said Jerilyn.

Lydia Grace sat on the floor and tore into it. When she opened the box she saw the beautiful

Betsy McCall doll with the curly brown hair. "She has hair like mine! Her head and legs and arms even move! She's got her own comb and brush. There's even a pattern included." She paused. "But I don't know how to sew."

Lily piped up, "You'll learn from Mom. She had me sewing when I was younger than you!"

"She's so beautiful. Thank you so much," said Lydia Grace, and she smiled from ear-to-ear as she hugged her parents, sisters, and brother.

Christopher stood. "I have an announcement to make before we head out for a light dinner and the Christmas Eve service at Christmas Hotel." Jerilyn stood on one side of him and the Scotts on the other. "Junior, Sadie, Willy, and Hazel, would you please stand?"

The bewildered children stood while looking at each other, questioning in their expressions as to what was happening. "I'm going to let Sheriff and Mrs. Scott take it from here."

Darius looked at the four children. "After many years of marriage, my wife and I have never been blessed with children, and we didn't know why until recently. The Lord tugged on my heart when I met you children. I think that He was waiting for us to meet all of you. If you will have us, we would like to be your parents."

"We promise to love you and protect you and be

the best parents we possibly can," added Barbara.

"Will you let us adopt you?" asked Darius.

The children looked from one to the other in amazement. Junior was the first to speak. "You want all ... *four* of us?"

The Scotts laughed. "Yes, we want all four of you," he said, while tousling Junior's hair. "We promise to treat you as the gifts from God that you are. If you'll all say yes, it will be the best Christmas ever for my wife and me. What do you say?"

The children looked from one to the other nodding to each other. The girls cried with happiness. Junior stepped forward. "We say yes, sir."

Darius and Barbara hugged each of the children.

Lydia Grace squealed the loudest in delight. "That was my second wish when I blew out my candles, and both wishes have come true! I have a home, and I wanted Junior, Sadie, Willy, and Hazel to have a home. This is going to be the best Christmas ever!"

Christopher hugged her. "I couldn't have said it better, my little angel."

*****

After dinner at Christmas Hotel, the family friends and hotel guests gathered in the hotel chapel with the Wright family. No electric lights were used on this night; only candles lit the room. Lily sat at the organ and was finishing playing the last Christmas hymn before Christopher addressed his congregation.

Christopher stood at his pulpit and gazed fondly toward his wife, their four children, and the Scotts with their newly acquired four children, many of the townspeople, and the guests of the hotel. Silently, he said a quick prayer.

He began to speak with the genuine love he felt for God, his family, and the people. "Tonight I'm reading the Christmas Story in Luke, which is a Christmas Eve tradition with my family. Then tomorrow morning, Saturday morning, for my Christmas sermon, we'll continue the story in Matthew, which actually takes place a couple of years later."

Taking a breath to try and calm his emotions, Christopher paused a moment. "Before I begin, I just want to give thanks to the Lord," he said, with some hoarseness in his voice. "Excuse me." He cleared his throat. He looked to Jerilyn for support, but her eyes were glistening, too. He turned back to his congregation. It was a small chapel, only six pews deep, and an aisle in the center. The chapel seated approximately ten on each of the twelve pews, and they were at full capacity. Many people were standing behind the last row and spilled into the lobby. The memories flooded his soul.

He removed his handkerchief from his breast pocket and wiped his eyes. "I have so many thoughts running through my head, and I feel very sentimental at the moment. Please bear with me. I can't possibly tell all of you the blessings that have occurred here at Christmas Hotel and in this little chapel over the years. Before I married my beloved wife Jerilyn, I baptized her in December, 1941 in the baptistery behind the altar where I stand. Although she had been saved when young, and then followed the Lord's direction in baptism at age eleven, she had newly rededicated her life to the Lord and wanted a fresh start. Jerilyn and I were married in this little chapel on New Year's Eve, 1941.

"So much has happened since then. Our oldest daughter Lily was saved and baptized at age eight. The twins Kenneth Elliot and Carrie Emeline were saved and baptized at ages nine and ten respectively." He paused again. "Then the only child Jerilyn and I conceived together, Lydia Grace, was kidnapped at birth from Protestant Hospital on Christmas morning in 1946. However, for you that do not already know, our dear Lydia Grace has been restored to us."

He gazed affectionately toward Lydia Grace. Jerilyn placed her arm around her daughter, brushed the hair back from her forehead, and gently kissed her forehead. The smiling crowd burst into applause. Handkerchiefs were removed from purses and breast pockets to dab at eyes and wipe the sniffles.

"Another blessing that has taken place this Christmas is for Sheriff Darius Scott and his wife Barbara. They've been married seventeen years and wanted a large family. It didn't appear it would happen. However, they never gave up hope. We all know the Lord in His infinite wisdom has His own timing." He looked fondly to his friends Darius and Barbara. Hazel and Willy were seated between them, with Junior beside Darius and Sadie beside Barbara. Darius and Barbara smiled at each of their four children and the children returned the smile to their new parents. Darius placed an arm around the two boys and Barbara did the same with the two girls. "The four children seated with them are their foster children whom they will adopt as their own, as soon as the court signs the papers." Then he chuckled, "I rather doubt that will take long. I think the sheriff has an inside track with Judge James."

The crowd laughed and applauded. They all turned to look at Judge James who was seated with his wife Nell and their children across the aisle from the Scotts. Judge James laughed good-naturedly and applauded, smiled, and nodded his head.

Before Christopher began the service, the congregation rose and sang 'O Come, All Ye Faithful,' 'O Little Town of Bethlehem' and 'silent Night' while Lily played the organ.

"Now, please remain standing for the reading of God's Word. Turn in your Bibles to Luke chapter two and I will read verses one through twenty."

*****

When the Christmas Eve service ended, Christopher stood in the doorway and thanked everyone for coming, and asked them to return at 11:00 am Saturday morning for the Christmas service. He reminded them that there would also be a Sunday morning service at 11:00 on December twenty-sixth. As they filed out, they shook his hand and thanked him for the lovely service. The Scotts remained behind.

Christopher spoke first. "Darius, I want you to know that Jerilyn and I can't thank you enough for organizing the search parties to try and bring our little girl home."

"Well, I think we're even. Barbara and I established a family from this ordeal. The Lord knew eight years ago how this would turn out. It gives even more meaning to Romans eight twenty-eight. I know I need to trust God's timing and not my own."

"I can't agree more," said Christopher. "If the six of you don't already have a noon meal planned tomorrow, Jerilyn, the children, and I would enjoy your company tomorrow here at Christmas Hotel for the Christmas meal following the service. I know that our chefs will be going all out with a festive banquet, and their families will be here, too."

Darius looked at Barbara who nodded her approval. "We'd be pleased to be here tomorrow. We'll open the presents as soon as the children awaken." He looked at the four children who returned his look in amazement. "Yes, the presents," chuckled Darius. "You didn't think we'd forget your first Christmas with us, did you? We also have a beautiful Douglas fir tree and the presents are already underneath. We just need to decorate the tree, which we can all do when we get home. Your belongings have already been moved to our home."

Sadie and Hazel began to cry and hugged their new parents. The boys hung their heads and discreetly wiped a tear.

"Come here, boys. You're not too big for a family hug."

They lifted their heads and walked into Darius and Barbara's welcoming arms.

*****

Later on that Christmas Eve evening, following the service and the caroling around town, the Wrights assembled in their living room around the Christmas tree and the piano for one last song. The family sang robustly and thoroughly enjoyed their first Christmas Eve evening together as a complete family. "Okay, it's bedtime," announced Jerilyn. "Actually it's two hours past your bedtime." She hugged each of her four children. "Don't get used to staying up so late." She laughed. "It's a special night, though. Sweet dreams!"

After the children were asleep, Jerilyn joined Christopher in the living room for a cup of spiced ginger Christmas tea. "Christopher, I think we need to address with Lydia Grace her anger toward Rose Clark. Tonight, she asked me if Rose went to Heaven because Rose stole her. I explained that Rose's sins were forgiven when she accepted Christ as her Lord and Savior. What do you think about taking a drive to Bowling Green and visiting Rose's grave tomorrow after church and following the noon meal?"

"I think that's a wonderful idea. In the meantime, let's pray about how to best get through to Lydia Grace. I think she needs to forgive Rose. This is only going to fester in her soul if she doesn't."

Chapter Twenty-Six

Forgiveness

"But they that wait upon the LORD shall renew their strength; they shall mount up with wings as eagles; they shall run, and not be weary; and they shall walk, and not faint."
Isaiah 40:31

Christmas morning
Saturday December 25, 1954
The excited children awakened Christopher and Jerilyn at 5:30 am. When Lydia Grace opened the huge box that contained a three-story doll house with a mom, dad, three girls, one boy, and a cocker spaniel dog, her shriek of delight filled the room. Jerilyn mouthed to Lily, Ken, and Carrie Emeline, "Good choice." After all, the three children had done the shopping for Lydia Grace for her birthday and Christmas. Lydia Grace also received her very own copy of *Charlotte's Web*.

The other three children had their share of excitement, too.

Ken received the extra track to enlarge his Lionel train set, along with more village people, trees, and buildings. He also received the newest

Hardy Boys story, *The Yellow Feather Mystery* to add to his Hardy Boys collection.

Lily received the book she asked for, *Freedom Train: The Story of Harriet Tubman*, and the much hoped-for University of Kentucky cheerleader's royal blue and white warm-up suit.

Carrie Emeline received the two books she wanted: the newest *Chronicles of Narnia* novel by C.S. Lewis, and *The Black Stallion's Sulky Colt* by Walter Farley. She also received a solid pastel pink button-down sweater, a pastel pink poodle skirt, and a solid pink blouse with a blue poodle appliqué on the upper left of the blouse near her collar. Pink was her favorite color.

After the Christmas service, the Wright family met the Scotts at Christmas Hotel for the Christmas banquet. The many chefs presented a grand feast, beginning with a Waldorf salad, a smoky butternut squash soup, ham, goose, asparagus casserole, oyster casserole, cornbread dressing, corn casserole, sweet potato casserole, and cranberry sauce; and for dessert, their choice of mincemeat pie, pumpkin pie, chess pie, or banana pudding.

The three older Wright children were used to the creations of the Christmas Hotel chefs, but Lydia Grace and the Smith children had never seen so much food in one place. All the new dishes were such a pleasure to their taste buds. The guests and townspeople who ate the Christmas meal thanked the chefs and the Wrights. Their friends Dr. Beasley and his wife and children, and Judge James and his wife and children, were also at the banquet and promised to attend the Sunday morning service.

*****

Immediately following the feast, the Wright family all piled in the station wagon. Christopher only told Lydia Grace they were going for a Sunday afternoon drive. "Since it's no longer snowing and windy, and the temperature is almost forty degrees, we thought today would be a good day."

The other children had been informed of the situation, and they had been praying for Lydia Grace. When they arrived at the cemetery in Bowling Green, Lydia Grace understood what was happening.

"I don't want to see her grave *ever again!*" she strongly announced in the first defiant moment that Christopher and Jerilyn had encountered with her. With her arms crossed in front of her she continued in rebellion, "She's not my mama anymore, and *never was!* She's a liar *and* a thief!"

Jerilyn and Christopher asked their three older children to go for a walk so they could sit in the back with Lydia Grace. The other children quietly walked away to give their parents time alone with their youngest sister.

When Christopher and Jerilyn were seated in the back seat on either side of Lydia Grace, she began to cry. Huge sobs racked her little body and her parents each placed a comforting arm around her and let her cry it out. "I thought she was my mama. I thought she *loved* me. She just used me to replace Lucy. She *stole* me. What was *wrong* with her? Didn't she know that stealing was *wrong*?"

"Lydia Grace," began Christopher, "all your points are valid. If I were in your shoes, I might feel the same way." He handed her his handkerchief.

"Really?" she asked as she sniffed and looked up at him.

"Yes, really. Rose Clark did something horrendous. However, at the time, she wasn't thinking straight. According to her letter to your mother and me, she was on the verge of killing herself. She was extremely depressed. She'd just lost her husband Leonard, whom she loved very much, and she'd lost the newborn baby daughter she carried in her womb for nine months. She didn't know the Lord Jesus, so she had no one with whom to discuss her situation. She was left with her own thoughts, and they were not happy thoughts.

"I think the night she kidnapped you, her mind snapped. She saw you, and you looked so much like her Lucy, and she wanted so much to be a mother. She followed her first instinct and that was to have you at all costs. When you were discovered missing, of course the hospital in Nashville reported it to the Nashville police and the Tennessee Sheriff's Department, but evidently they didn't suspect Rose, and she was over seventy miles away across the state border in Bowling Green, Kentucky. After Mommy and I came home from the hospital, we subscribed to the *Nashville Banner* newspaper for a long time, but there was no mention of a suspect. The kidnapping case grew cold.

"However, I believe all the time Rose Clark was raising you, she knew it was wrong. In her letter, she talked about sometimes bringing you to Christmas Hotel. When she saw your mommy and me, she knew what she'd done was dreadfully wrong. I believe her sin was eating at her physical wellbeing.

"Rose was saved from her sins last August. Barbara Scott, the church secretary, said she was baptized by their pastor shortly afterwards. Mrs. Scott told us she remembered typing the certificate of baptism when we met with her while we were looking for you, and we later found it in her Bible with the two letters she wrote. Because Rose became a Christian, she was forgiven of her sins. If the Lord can forgive Rose ... can't you, honey?" he said softly.

"Do you think she's in Heaven with Jesus?"

asked Lydia Grace.

"I know she is. The Bible literally says when we as Christians are absent from the body, we are present with the Lord. That means that when a Christian dies, his or her spirit immediately dwells with the Lord Jesus."

"Will she see her husband and real baby again?"

"I pray she's with them now, honey. The Bible says the Lord will eventually wipe away our tears. I believe that means that there will no longer be sadness in Heaven. Therefore, Rose will no longer be sad about what she did to you, and your mommy, and me either. She will no longer fret about her sins. Her sins have been forgiven."

"Have you and Mommy forgiven her?" Lydia Grace looked from one to the other.

"It was hard at first, but I can honestly say that I have, honey," answered Jerilyn.

"I have, too," said Christopher softly. "Rose is my sister in Christ."

Lydia Grace turned to Jerilyn and then Christopher, and said, "I can forgive her if you can."

Christopher and Jerilyn each hugged their daughter. "Let's get out of this car and visit her grave," said Christopher. "Your mommy and I brought a poinsettia from Christmas Hotel. The pot is in the back, if you'd like to place it on her grave."

"Okay," she said.

They all got out, closed the doors, and Christopher swung open the rear door to the station wagon. He handed the pot to Lydia Grace. They walked beside her as she carried the Poinsettia to Rose's grave, and the other three children followed. A prayer had been answered. Lydia Grace had now forgiven Rose Clark.

Chapter Twenty-Seven

Protector and Shield

*"But thou, O LORD, art a shield for me; my
glory, and the lifter up of mine head. I cried
unto the LORD with my voice, and he heard me
out of his holy hill. Selah.
I laid me down and slept; I awaked; for the
LORD sustained me."*
Psalms 3:3-5

Sunday morning
December 26, 1954
Christopher was finishing the delivery of his
Sunday morning sermon on Psalms 3:3-5, in the
chapel of Christmas Hotel. Lydia Grace hung on
every word as the sermon spoke to her heart. She
thought about the night she spent at the fountain in
Bowling Green, Kentucky, and how she had prayed
to the Baby Jesus on December first, in front of the
Methodist church.

Lydia Grace was quiet when she left the chapel
with her parents. She did not say much at the noon
meal in Christmas Hotel's dining room, either.

When they arrived back home, Lily and the twins went to their rooms to enjoy a Sunday afternoon reading of their Christmas books, while Lydia Grace sought out her parents who were having coffee in the living room. The tree was lit, and Lydia Grace studied the bubble lights in fascination before standing on the threshold watching her parents. *Her* parents, she thought. *Thank You, God, for my real parents.*

Christopher looked up and saw Lydia Grace in the doorway. "Would you like to sit with us, honey?"

She walked toward them, and Jerilyn moved over on the sofa so she could sit between them.

After she was settled, she looked from one to the other. "I listened to the sermon this morning, and the words caused me to remember. I thought about the day that the woman I loved and thought was my mama died, and it was also the day I thought it was my birthday. I had no place to go and I was cold and hungry. I stopped in front of the Methodist church and looked down at the Baby Jesus. After a while I prayed. I asked the Baby Jesus if He knew that my mama had died and if He knew it was my birthday. I wanted the Baby Jesus to know I was alone, and I asked for Him to help me. I told Him I was cold and I asked Him if He would protect me, and did He know someone out there who might love me. I was so scared." Her chin quivered, but she held back the tears.

"I went to the fountain to try and find some shelter, but I was so cold. I finally fell asleep counting the stars. When I woke up, I was cold again, but Bullet came and lay down behind me and kept me warm. I was no longer alone, and I was warm. It was like that verse you preached about this morning. How does it go again?"

"I believe you mean Psalms three and verses three to five. *'But thou, O Lord, art a shield for me; my glory, and the lifter up of mine head. I cried unto the Lord with my voice, and he heard me out of his holy hill. I laid me down and slept; I awaked; for the Lord sustained me.'* Is that what you mean?"

"Yes, that's it! He really does hear us, doesn't He, Daddy?"

"Yes, honey, He does. Jesus came to earth as a baby to save us from our sins. He is our protector, like Bullet was your protector, but unlike Bullet He will never die. He will always be here for you. Jesus is eternal. Do you want Jesus to save you, honey, so you can be with Jesus forever?"

"Yes, Daddy, but how?"

"I know that Rose.... Now that you have forgiven her, why don't we call her Mama Rose? How does that sound?"

"That's perfect," and she smiled. "I really didn't know what to call her."

"Her name will come up in the future, so Mama Rose it is. And now back to your question. I know Mama Rose took you to church, but I don't know how much you've learned and what you believe. Do you believe in your heart that Jesus can forgive your sins, and then allow you to live with Him forever?"

"Yes, Daddy, I believe that."

"Do you believe Jesus died on the cross for your sins and rose to Heaven three days later?"

"Yes, Mrs. Scott taught us about that in Sunday school. She said He could forgive all our past sins and our future sins." She hung her head. "Sometimes I didn't always tell Mama Rose the truth. Sometimes I was late coming home from school, because I was watching the television at Lerman's Department Store. On Saturday I would sneak out to watch the *Roy Rogers Show*. I didn't always tell my Mama Rose the truth about where I was. I just loved to watch *his* Bullet. He looked just like *my* Bullet. Did you know that's why I named him Bullet?"

Christopher laughed and nodded. "We suspected that, honey."

She smiled and then her expression sobered. "Mama Rose would ask me why I was late, and I didn't tell her I was watching the television at the store. That was a lie. If I ask Jesus to forgive my sins, will He really forgive the lies I told?"

"Yes, He will. Jesus will come into your heart and change your life. You'll be able to leave your broken unchangeable past of the last eight years in His hands, and meet the future that the Lord has planned for you. Accepting the Lord Jesus today as your Lord and Savior will change your life for the better, and forever. Is that what you want to do, honey?"

"Yes, Daddy."

"Well, let's all hold hands, close our eyes, and you ask Him in your own words."

Lydia Grace closed her eyes and prayed aloud, "Dear Jesus, I've been bad at times and I want to ask You to forgive me, because I really *am* sorry. I didn't always tell the truth. I've recently held bad thoughts about Mama Rose, and I'm sorry. I know that only You can save me, and I ask You to come into my heart and save me from my sins. I know You died on the cross for my sins, and I know You're in Heaven with Your Father. I know You love me, and You will save me, and I'll live with You forever. Thank You, Jesus. I love You, too. Thank You for sending Bullet and Mr. Gabe to protect me. Thank You for bringing me home to my real family. Please tell Mama Rose that I forgive her. Amen."

Christopher and Jerilyn hugged her. "That was beautiful, honey," Christopher said. He saw the tears glistening in Jerilyn's eyes. Then he looked up and said, "Thank You, Lord."

Chapter Twenty-Eight

The Gift

"Beloved, if God so loved us, we ought also to love one another."
1 John 4:11

February 20, 1955
through April 02, 1955
On a blustery snowy morning, two months later, Ruth ran across South College Street to make an announcement. "Bonnie had six puppies!"

Lydia Grace's eyes grew huge. "Can we see them?" she asked.

"Well, their mama is still cleaning them, and sometimes the mama is nervous when her puppies are first born and doesn't like visitors. Let's wait until their eyes open, which will be about nine or ten days." Ruth needed to make certain the puppies were healthy and would live. She didn't want Lydia Grace upset so soon after Bullet's death. She also wanted to wait and see the sex of one particular puppy.

Every day Lydia Grace looked at the kitchen calendar. Jerilyn had marked when nine days was up. On the ninth day, Lydia Grace rose early, one hour before breakfast. "Do you think their eyes are open yet?" she asked with such excitement that she could hardly sit still.

"Well, let's call Ruth's mom," suggested Jerilyn.

It was a weekday and Ruth was at Western Kentucky University during the week. However, Ruth's mother Irene answered. "Irene, this is Jerilyn. Well, good morning to you, too. Lydia Grace has been counting off nine days to see if the puppy's eyes might be open. Have you had a chance to look at them this morning? ... Okay. .. All right. ... Well, we'll wait until you call us, and thank you." She hung up the phone.

She turned to Lydia Grace. "All six puppies are doing fine, and four have their eyes open. She suggested that we wait for the other two puppies. She also said Bonnie is still nervous with visitors. She would like us to wait until Friday night when Ruth gets home. She said that Bonnie is much calmer around Ruth."

"All right, Mommy," Lydia Grace said, clearly with disappointment.

"In the meantime, you can help me with breakfast. If you'll get a dozen eggs from the refrigerator, I'll start frying some bacon."

*****

Three days later, on Friday evening after dinner, Ruth called. Jerilyn answered the phone. "Hi, Ruth.

... No, we're not busy. ... Yes, we can come over. Do you mean now? ... Okay, thank you. I think that would be just fine."

Jerilyn saw the hopeful look from her youngest daughter. "Yes, honey, we've all been invited to visit the puppies. Ruth says you could even hold one of them."

"Yippee!" Lydia Grace shrieked with happiness.

Fifteen minutes later, the Wright family, except for Lily who had returned to school, was on Ruth's front porch ringing the bell.

The family was escorted back to the warm kitchen where Bonnie lay in a box with old towels, rags, and her puppies.

"Oh, they're so cute!" Lydia Grace squealed with laughter as she looked at the puppies. Four of them were nursing and two were sleeping. The two families watched Lydia Grace as she studied the puppies. She pointed to one of the fat sleeping pups, and said in amazement, "That one looks just like Bullet."

"I know," said Ruth softly. "We're certain that Bullet is the daddy to these puppies. He was the only dog Bonnie made friends with in December. That puppy is a little boy. Is he the one you'd like to hold?" she asked cautiously.

"Oh, may I?"

Ruth picked up the sleeping puppy and Lydia

Grace sat cross-legged on the floor, making certain she didn't drop this precious puppy. Ruth placed it in Lydia Grace's hands while the families watched. What Lydia Grace didn't know was Ruth had already asked Jerilyn earlier if she could give the puppy to Lydia Grace. They agreed that if Lydia Grace wanted the puppy, she could have him when he was old enough to leave Bonnie.

Lydia Grace stroked the puppy that now nestled on her lap. He woke up, yawned and went back to sleep. The families watched Lydia Grace to make sure she was okay. Lydia Grace never raised her head, but they saw a tear fall from her eye and splash on the puppy.

Jerilyn sat down on the floor and placed her arm around her daughter's shoulders.

"I'm okay, Mommy," said Lydia Grace, sounding very mature for her eight years. She looked up at her mommy, and Jerilyn saw more tears threatening to spill over. "These aren't sad tears, they're happy tears. I was just thinking that these puppies were alive in Bonnie's tummy when Bullet was still alive. Then I thought about you and me. I was in your tummy a long time before I was born. Bullet was with these puppies before he died, and you were with me before I was kidnapped. Because of Bullet these puppies are here, and because of you and Daddy, I'm here. Isn't God amazing?"

Jerilyn looked at Christopher and the twins and saw three pairs of tear-filled eyes. She kissed her daughter's cheek. "Yes, honey, God *is* amazing."

Ruth knelt down beside Jerilyn and Lydia Grace. "Lydia Grace, since I'm at school during the week, will you help me find homes for the other five?"

"Yes," Lydia Grace said cautiously, "but ... but what about *this* puppy? Does ... does he already have a home?" she asked in a quivering voice.

"Yes, I believe he does. I talked to your mommy, and he has a home with you ... if you want him? Do you want him?"

"Oh, yes, thank you! I want him!" she cried with happiness.

"Well, you'll have to start thinking about a name for him," said Jerilyn.

"I will, Mommy. I'll think of a really special name." Then she looked back at Ruth. "I'll also start asking some of my new friends in Franklin if they want a puppy. May I visit him while you're at school?"

"I think that can be arranged. Bonnie is much better now about having visitors. I don't think I'll need to be here anymore. When your puppy is six weeks old, you can take him home. How does that sound?"

"Great! I'm going to go home and mark the calendar."

The puppy woke up and began to make little whimpering puppy sounds. "I think he's hungry," said Lydia Grace. The other sleeping pup had awakened while Lydia Grace held this pup and it was now nursing with the other four. "We'd better give him back to his mommy."

Ruth picked up the puppy and placed him at his mama's breast. "She sure has a lot of breasts," said Lydia Grace matter-of-factly. Both families laughed and Jerilyn hugged her.

Lydia Grace visited the pup every day after school, and marked the calendar for Sunday, April third. The puppies grew and played and were eating soft food at four weeks. In the meantime, Lydia Grace was asking her new school friends about homes for the other five pups. Although her pup looked just like a German Shepherd, four of the pups looked like a combination of a Collie and a German Shepherd. However, there was one male that looked just like Bonnie.

On Saturday, March 26, Nettie Sue, along with Booker, little Jimmy, and little Robert were in town shopping. Jerilyn and Lydia Grace were shopping, too. Lydia Grace told the boys about the puppies, and they wanted to see them. As soon as they saw the male pup that looked just like a Collie, they asked their parents if they could have him. Nettie Sue just laughed and said, "One more dog won't hurt anything on the farm."

Ruth said the puppy would be ready to leave in one week. Therefore, if they were in town the following Saturday, the pup could go home with them. Three-year-old Robert laughed with joy, and clapped his hands with the news.

"We'll be back next Saturday," said Nettie Sue.

"Does that mean I can have my puppy a day early, too?" asked Lydia Grace.

"It's fine with me," said Ruth. "One day won't hurt. However, we've still got four more pups that need homes."

"I know, and I've told all my friends. Some just said they needed to ask their parents. They know they need to wait six weeks, so they'll probably come and look at them next week.

*****

Saturday, April second finally arrived, and Lydia Grace was again up early. "We'll have breakfast before we pick up your puppy," said Jerilyn. "While I cook, go down to the basement and find a cardboard box and an old quilt or some rags to make him a bed."

She returned with the requested items, and the family ate breakfast. Lydia Grace couldn't sit still, she was too excited. Even Ken and Carrie Emeline were anxious for their little sister. They were excited to bring the puppy home, too.

As soon as the dishes were washed, Jerilyn called and asked Ruth if now would be a convenient time to pick up the puppy. Ruth told them to come on over.

When they arrived, three of the pups were missing. "You were right, Lydia Grace," said Ruth. "Three of your friends were here this morning. When you take your puppy and the McLemore boys take theirs, we'll only have one left. Thank you so much for your help."

"You're welcome," she replied.

Ruth reached down in the box and handed Lydia Grace her puppy. Lydia Grace had to sit down, because he wiggled and licked her face and hands. She laughed while playing on the floor with the puppy.

The McLemore family showed up to pick up their pup. Robert sat on the floor with his pup and said, "We're going to call him Tony!"

They all laughed along with the precocious little boy in his excitement.

"Have you chosen a name for your puppy?" Ruth asked Lydia Grace.

"Yes, I have." She looked at her parents because she had not told them. "I'd like to call him Gabe, if Mommy and Daddy think it would be okay with Mr.

Gabe."

Christopher paused, nodded his head, and answered, "I think Mr. Gabe would be pleased."

"Enjoy your puppies," Ruth said to the little ones.

"I know I will," responded Lydia Grace. "Thank you, Ruth."

That was little Robert's cue, "Thank you, Ruth," he said.

"You're both quite welcome," Ruth replied.

Lucy smiled at her family and friends. It's good to be home, she thought.

Epilogue

"And I will bring the blind by a way that they knew not; I will lead them in paths that they have not known: I will make darkness light before them, and crooked things straight. These things will I do unto them, and not forsake them."
Isaiah 42:16

In early January, 1955, Barbara Scott read a story in the *Bowling Green Daily News* about a hunter who had found a dead German Shepherd dog in the woods about a half mile from the square. The hunter noticed the bullet wound and assumed that the dog had been accidentally shot by a hunter. He said it was the biggest dog he ever saw.

In March, 1955 Otto and Eula Mae Smith were each charged with five counts of child abuse and each was sentenced to ten years in prison. Otto was sent to the Kentucky State Reformatory in Oldham County, Kentucky, and Eula Mae was incarcerated at the Kentucky Correctional Institution for Women in Shelby County, Kentucky. Their four children were now stable and secure, as the adopted children of Darius and Barbara Scott.

On a lovely spring day during Lily's Easter vacation, the Wright family drove to the Nashville City Cemetery to visit the graves of Rose's husband Leonard and her daughter Lucille Grace. Lydia Grace placed flowers on each grave. Before the summer ended, Christopher and Jerilyn made arrangements to have the bodies exhumed and reburied beside Rose.

On September 25, 1955 Christopher Joseph Wright Jr. is born.

In December, 1955, when Lily arrives home from college for Christmas break, the Wright family has their group Christmas portrait made at *Bryant's Studio* on North Main near *Massey Motor Company* to include Lydia Grace, Christopher Joseph Wright Jr., Daisy, and Gabe.

About Saundra Staats McLemore

Saundra Staats McLemore is a member of the American Christian Fiction Writers (ACFW) and the Ohio chapter of the ACFW. Saundra is also a member of Landmark Baptist Church in Dayton, Ohio. After thirty-three years, Saundra is recently retired as President/CEO of McLemore & Associates, Inc., a nationwide sales and marketing business she built in 1984.

Saundra's passion has always been history, and she enjoys reading historical Christian fiction. Saundra's novel *Abraham and Anna* was endorsed by two of her favorite authors: Richard Paul Evans (author of *The Christmas Box*) and Jeanette Oke (author of the Love Comes Softly series). Saundra has two series published: The two-book inspirational eighteenth century Staats Family Chronicles and the six-book inspirational Christmas Hotel series. Saundra is currently writing her ninth novel: *For the Love of Ali.*

Born and raised in the state of Ohio, Saundra is married to Robert, and Anthony is their only child.

The other two members of the family are the cat Charley, and the mixed-Treeing Walker Coonhound Sadie.

Email: sstaatsmclemore@aol.com
Web site: http://www.saundrastaatsmclemore.com

Author's notes

Although all my books are works of fiction, I do like some real people to "visit" my stories.

Little Robert McLemore grew up to be my wonderful husband. His collie Tony was the first dog in his memory that lived on the family farm; therefore, I decided to insert the collie in the story. Again, I thank Robert for his patience, as I pursue the passion I have to write inspirational stories. Robert was a 1970 graduate of Franklin-Simpson High School in Franklin, Kentucky, and attended the University of Kentucky and Western University following high school.

Nettie Sue Harris McLemore currently resides in Bowling Green, Kentucky, but James E. (Booker) McLemore has been deceased since 1994. Jimmy McLemore was a veteran of the Vietnam War and has been deceased since 1990. Nettie Sue's parents Roy Harris and Josie (Mama) Harris are both deceased.

Mr. Davidson on Morris Street was my husband's step-grandfather on his father's side of the family.

He was Franklin, Kentucky's butcher for many years.

The Christmas Hotel Series was inspired by an article from January, 2008, in the Franklin Favorite, the newspaper in Franklin, KY. The article spoke about a diary left behind in the now razed Keystop Motel in Franklin, KY. The diary, dated 1873, possibly belonged to a young girl named C.E. Bazell from Rock Camp, Ohio. An Ohio assistant librarian traced the diary to a girl named Carrie E. Bazell who lived in Rock Camp with her parents until the late 1800s. Carrie Bazell died March 20, 1884 at the age of twenty-one, according to a brief obituary.

For all my readers of many different denominations, I chose the Methodist Church on State Street, not to promote the Methodist church denomination, but because that particular church was present in 1954 and near Fountain Square Park.

Look for *Christmas Redemption*, set in Franklin, Kentucky, the third book in the Christmas Hotel Series, December 20, 2018.

At this writing:

Child Abuse Information:
www.reportchildabusenow.com
www.childhelp.org/
1-800-4- A- Child (1-800-422-4453)

Depression Hotline: 1-630-482-9696
Suicide hotline: 1-800-784-8433

National Drug & Alcohol Treatment Hotline
800-662-HELP

Trust in the LORD with all thine heart; and lean not unto thine own understanding. In all thy ways acknowledge him, and he shall direct thy paths (Proverbs 3: 5-6).

A sneak peek at the third book in the Christmas Hotel series: *Christmas Redemption*. Enjoy!

Chapter One

Cecilia

"And for this cause God shall send them strong delusion, that they should believe a lie:"
2 Thessalonians 2:11

Houston, Texas
December 1, 1967
The cab driver turned in his seat and asked Cecilia if she was sure she wanted to go to the address she had given him. He had a kind face and his voice resonated concern, but his brow was furrowed with uncertainty. The name on his picture identification read Thomas Woodson.

Donna, a school friend, had given her the dubious address, and had merely said, "The doctor will take care of *it*." Cecilia said nothing, but nodded to the driver, and continued to look out the window. Mr. Woodson sped off to the other side of town; the seedy side of town. Although Cecilia entered the cab from Donna's apartment, she passed by the homes in her parents' middle class neighborhood, and then crossed the downtown business district.

They entered a rundown neighborhood to which she had never been. People stood and stared as her taxi drove past. Cecilia assumed taxis were a rare occurrence. She and her driver rode together in silence. From the corner of her eye she sensed him sometimes glancing back at her through the rearview mirror.

After a forty minute drive, Mr. Woodson stopped the car and turned to her again. "Miss, I just want to ask you one more time. Are you certain you want to be here? You can change your mind." His voice rang with so much concern that for a brief instant she considered taking his advice.

Cecilia gazed at the rundown building from the cab window. She looked down and checked the slip of paper, verifying the address. The address matched what was on the outside of the building. She turned back to the driver. In a thin voice she did not recognize as her own, she said, "I'm sure." The meter had stopped clicking each new amount. After checking the meter to view her fare, she opened her purse and counted out $4.30 plus a $1.00 tip.

"Thank you, Miss. Here's my card with my number. If you change your mind, call me, and I'll come back. There's a phone booth on that corner." He pointed in the direction. Cecilia's gaze followed the imaginary line to its destination, where a red booth sat near a park bench. An unshaved and shivering man wrapped in a threadbare blanket lay on the bench. "If you'll call me, I won't even charge you for the return ride. I know what they do in there."

She accepted his card, thanked him, and deposited it in her purse. He opened her door, and she stepped out clutching her purse. Mr. Woodson reached in, grabbed the small suitcase off the back seat, and handed it to her.

"I'll call you when I'm finished," she said in a determined, but soft voice. She stood straight, squared her thin shoulders, strode to the front door, and knocked.

A middle-aged woman wearing a stained uniform opened the door. "What's your name?" she asked in a gruff voice.

"My name is Cecilia Edmondson."

"You're late. Come in, Miss Edmondson. The doctor is expecting you."

Cecilia turned her head and noted the taxi driver was still at the curb. She turned back to the woman and entered the dilapidated building.

*****

Christmas Redemption will be available December 20, 2018. Authors depend on reviews. Please leave a review for *Christmas for Lucy: A Child's Quest for Love* on the distributor's website, and thank you!

Made in the USA
Middletown, DE
14 December 2019